the
BOOKWORM
box

Helping the community, one book at a time

AWAY FROM HERE

CHRISTOPHER HARLAN

Contents

Away From Here
By Christopher Harlan

Cover design, Formatting, and teaser designs by Jessica
Hildreth
Edited by Jessica Kempker

Reviews of Away From Here

"Reading this book moved me in a way no other book has done before. I laughed out loud, I teared up, I smiled, and I suffered heartbreak right along with Logan and Annalise. I could see a little of myself in both of them, and I know you will too. Away From Here will stay with me forever, no doubt. This book is not just a Young Adult novel. It's for everyone."
   ---Shelly

"What a wonderful YA story!!! But I don't want everyone to think it's only a YA story because it's an everybody story. I knew when I was 3% in and already crying it was going to be good...I had indeed fell into the rabbit hole of this book not to be seen again until I was finished with this book. What a wonderful YA story for this author."
   ---Misti

"The way the author laid out the ups and downs of that first love, albeit one skewed by many other issues going on inside the homes of each character, it gave a glimpse of how a teenage mind processes and understands their first love. The story, for me, was about more than the mental illness Logan's character and Anna's character were both experiencing at home and carrying into a relationship it was about how one person can inspire and save another from going down the same path they see at home... This book is amazing, from the beginning to the end and I hated finishing it because I wanted to stay in that story longer. All good things come to an end. I recommend this book for everyone, it isn't just for young adults, I think it is a book for everyone to get something out of. 10/10"

---Anna

"This book is so much more than a Young Adult Novel. It's a reflection of all of us...Our struggles, our happiness, our strength to move on from disappointments to be a stronger person. I can easily identify myself with the characters because I've been there and I still am. One thing I learned from this book is, that mental illness is nothing to be ashamed of. It lingers in all of us in one shape or form; some just struggle more than others. In the end we learn to cope with our feelings and learn from the experience.

On a personal note. I will gift this book to my teenage daughter. As a recovering addict who struggles with self-esteem issues I think she can learn a lot from this book and hopefully take some great feedback with her. This book made me look back at my teenage years, laugh and cry. I was barely into the first chapter when tears already took over. What an incredible read for all ages."

--- Michaela

"What can I say about "Away From Here"? It is personal, emotional, refreshing, and made me reflect upon the journey we all take through life. Logan and Anna became friends when they needed each other the most and for a while, all of their problems seemed to fade just a little bit. Christopher Harlan is truly a gifted and passionate writer and I know this book will be in my heart forever."

   ---Lisa

"What an emotional Ya novel that stomps on your soul forever. If you love stories about how a character tells you about his first love ..then this is definitely a book you must read. The author nailed this book bringing so many emotions I had to put it down and just breathe. Definitely in my top Ya reads for 2018 5/5 stars."

   ---Paula

"Harlan brings a wit and almost stream of consciousness feel to the prose. His ability to move freely from speaking directly to the reader, to keeping the flow of the story makes this a unique type of read. The characters are genuine and feel like these people could be your classmates from back when. In addition, the discussion of mental health issues, not only being totally relevant is dealt with in such a careful, honest, moving way. This is a deep read that requires time and attention as there is much detail that should not be missed."

   ---Lg

"Mr. Harlan's words brought them all back to me as I read Logan's story. There was also a very real view of mental illness and depression and how teenagers deal with it. Whether they are suffering from it or a loved one is, dealing with it in your teenage years is a confusing and difficult time. Mr. Harlan did an awesome job depicting some difficult situations. The story is told from Logan's point of view which was light most of the times and very to the point. He was very relatable and I fell in love with his story. It was a great read"

---Christine

"I would definitely recommend this book. Thank you Mr. Harlan for the ways you seem to have reached into my memories and write about things that are my secrets but now seem to be the same secrets others have too."

---Lori

"I highly recommend this YA novel. It is for everyone really. From those who want a love story, to those who want to remember what being a teen was like, even teens who want to know if they are the only ones out there who feel so "bleh." It is a definite must read."

---Meghan

"Away from here is such a tender and moving teen love story showing what it's like in the real world. Anyone with a heart and compassion should read this and love it as much as I did. Christopher Harlan is right on the mark with this one"

---Susan

"This book is a rollercoaster of emotions from start to finish, even though it's a YA it in no way effected the way I felt reading it. The author tapped into a range of feelings that at times left me tearful, but so glad I read it. so high praise to Christopher for trying a new genre and in my eyes smashed it!"

---Janine

"I haven't read a YA book in almost 10 years and even as an adult this book spoke to me. To the author, what an amazing job you did with this story…"
---Elizabeth

Foreword

The relationship between our greatest strengths and our
greatest weaknesses has always been something that interested me, probably because the most formative experiences
of my life have surrounded witnessing the complexity of
that relationship. Like our main character, Logan, I was a
nerdy, mixed up mixed kid who grew up in a house
haunted by mental illness. But in that same household I
witnessed the kind of strength, toughness, and resilience
that made me the man I am today. The contrast between
those two forces was the inspiration for this book. I wanted
to explore the complexity of flawed and powerful women
through the eyes of the teenaged boy who's been influenced by them, and one who's experiencing the over-
whelming power of his first love.

This isn't strictly autobiographical. To fictionalize the
exact experiences of my adolescence would have been
interesting, but ultimately confining. There was no
Annalise for me when I was that lonely kid. There were
comics, to be sure, and a best friend for the ages, but alas,
no actual girl. I hope that in reading Logan and Annalise's

story that you'll discover (or rediscover) elements that harken to experiences in your own life, and that through Logan's eyes you'll remember the particular intensity of being a teenager that we oftentimes forget as adults.

I never knew Annalise, she's an invention of my mind, but my nerdy, teenaged boy self would have given away every number 1 Marvel Comic I owned (no small collection btw) to have had a girl like her in my life at the time. So enjoy the story. When you meet Logan, tell him I said *what's up*, and that I'll return his Uncanny X-men graphic novel shortly. And when you run into Our Girl, remind her that she's anything but ordinary.

---Christopher, 2018

Synopsis

When I was seventeen years old there were only three things that I knew for certain: I was a mixed up mixed kid, with weird hair and an unhealthy love of comics; I wanted to forget I'd ever heard the words depression and anxiety; and I was hopelessly in love with a girl named Annalise who was, in every way that you can be, a goddess. What can I say about Anna? She wasn't the prom queen or the perfect girl from the movies, she was my weird, funny, messed up goddess. The girl of my dreams. The reason I'm writing these words.

I'd loved Anna from a distance, afraid to actually talk to her, but then one day during lunch my best friend threw a french fry at my face and changed everything. The rest, as they say, is history. Our History. Our Story. Annalise helped make me the man I am today, and loving her saved my teenaged soul from drowning in the depths of a terrible *Bleh*, the worst kind of sadness that there is, a concept Anna taught me about a long time ago, when we were younger than young.

So flip the book over, open up the cover and let me tell

you Our Story, which is like Annalise, herself: complicated, beautiful, funny, and guaranteed to teach you something by the time you're through. Maybe it'll teach you the complexity of the word potato, something I never understood until the very last page.

Dedication

To all the girls who could have been Annalise – remember that hope isn't just for suckers, and that you're anything but ordinary.
To the honorary members of the Kids of Sick Parents Club—I know you're out there—just hold on tight until you can see the horizon, it comes eventually, I promise you. Share your stories with anyone who'll listen.
To all the women whose strength, vulnerability, and self-sacrifice remains a thing of wonder to me – I'll never cease to be amazed by you.
This is for you all.

Prologue

I remember a time before you cried every night, a time before you shook every morning.

I remember a lot of things, even though I'm only seventeen years old. I guess I'm like those people who were alive when the Internet was first invented. I'm like them because I also saw the shift, the turning point, the world before and after. I remember the night when Dad finally decided he'd had enough of all this and walked out the door, never to return again. I think deep down you blamed yourself for his leaving, but fathers and husbands leave sometimes, Mom, no matter how much you want them to stay. I guess they get to do what sons and daughters don't. They get to make a choice as to whether or not they want to deal with nights like tonight; nights when I can hear you sobbing through both of our closed doors.

It frightens me that I'm so used to it.

I don't ask what's wrong because I know what's wrong. Everything's wrong, isn't it? It's on nights like these that I go to the window in our bathroom and pray to a God I don't even know if I believe in. I don't know why I do it, but even though I'm not religious, I clasp my hands and pray. I pray for a lot of things: for you to be better, for me to be able to have a life outside of these walls, and for the chance to meet *her*.

I don't know who or where she is, but I pray that one day she'll come to take me away from Here.

Note

_____

The occasional and Seemingly Random Capitalization of Some words in the Story is intentional, and Not Random at all, so don't Worry.

"Yeah, I know just what you're sayin'
    And I regret ever complainin'
    About this heart and all its breakin'
    It was beauty we were making"
    ---Sam Smith, *Palace*

"It's never the changes we want that change everything."

"Dude wore his nerdiness like a Jedi wore his light saber. .
.Couldn't have passed for Normal if he'd wanted to."

---Junot Diaz, *The Brief Wondrous Life of Oscar Wao*

Part One

Where I finally speak to the girl of my dreams, I learn the complexities of the word potato, and I begin a whole new chapter in what was, at that point, a sad, miserable excuse for an adolescent boy's life. . . . so, yeah. . . Bleh.

Two flowers on your forearm, one smaller and one larger.

Two flowers to cover the bad things you did to yourself that time you forgot that you're the only reason the sun rises each morning. Scars are storytellers, aren't they? They're like that wise, old dude in the park who you know has some good stories to tell, if only someone would ask him about those days when he wasn't yet an old dude. But no one ever does. Scars are like that. They're the old guy in the park no one talks to. But yours are adorned with flowers.

New life.

Renewal.

Rejuvenation.

Your scars are painted with new skin and pretty colors of your own choosing.

Your scars will heal.

And one day, if anyone ever asks about them, you won't even remember how they got there.

ONE

Where I tell you all about that beautiful Peruvian goddess who rescued my soul.

According to the *Council of They*, those unnamed shadow experts who we cite whenever we start a sentence with *they say* (come on, you know you do it all the time), the opening line of any book might be the most important, so here goes mine: in the fall of my senior year of high school, I fell madly in love with a girl name Annalise, who saved my miserable teenaged soul from a fate most foul. That sounded dramatic, right? Exaggeration 101? No embell-ishment, just the truth, so help me. That's the first time I've mentioned her by name, isn't it? Annalise. Our Girl.

I was going through some serious stuff at the start of senior year, and I was about as mixed up as a mixed kid gets. I know, hardly groundbreaking news, right? No need to alert the church elders when a teenager is a little screwed up. Normal. Typical. Ordinary. I get it, but listen, my life at the time was anything but ordinary, trust me. I mean, yeah, there was all the normal stuff you'd expect: college loomed on the horizon like an invading army, teachers were getting more annoying with each passing class, and I was struggling to keep my grades up where they needed to be. I was typical in those ways.

But in my case there was much more than that going on behind the scenes. At the time Our Story begins, my sad teenaged soul was drowning in the depths of a terrible *Bleh*, a concept Annalise first introduced me to, and one I'll elaborate on in a little bit. But for right now, think of it as representing the darkest recesses of the human experience, encompassing a range of negative emotions from your run-of-the mill crappy day, all the way to the deepest abyss of human darkness.

So why was I in that state? Well, a few years before I met Anna, my parents finally decided to euthanize a rapidly devolving marriage. In the packing of my father's suitcase that followed the screaming and hateful words, my life became collateral damage, that poor bastard who's standing next to the terrorist right before the drone strike hits.

After Dad decided he'd had enough of us, mom's neurotransmitters got up to their old tricks and gave the middle finger to Serotonin, and the daily routine of uncontrollable tremors and crying began. Her days, which became *my* days, went something like this: crying and trembling in the morning before getting Xanax down the hatch; depressed catatonia around lunchtime, sometimes accompanied by a nap, sometimes without; a little more crying in the evening, and finally a trip to bed to retire for the night after watching a little too much mindless TV. Now imagine what I just said, if you can, and multiply that experience by days, weeks, months, years. You get the idea. So between the rapid descent of my home into some kind of madness never before seen by the eyes of man, and my natural tendency towards all things weird and dark, it was a less than ideal way to start my last year of high school.

But wait, we haven't been properly introduced yet, have we? My name is Logan Santiago, Logan Rosario Santiago to be exact. How Hispanic do I sound, *Jesus*! It's a mutt's name, like your narrator himself, the fulfilment of immigrant dreams from Southern Europe and the Caribbean, all of which found each other in the same place all immigrant dreams met up in Twentieth century America – Queens, New York. So, anyway, I'm Logan, and I'll be your fake Spanish narrator. I've called myself fake Spanish my whole life because the truth is, although my mom spoke it as her first language, I didn't learn a word outside of a few phrases that no rational person would call fluency. No matter if my name made it sound like I was straight outta San Juan, within the community, if you can't speak the language you might as well call yourself Bob Smith from Duluth, Minnesota. Fake Spanish all the way.

So what did I do? How did I handle this next level stress and anxiety I was feeling 24/7? I started a club. I know, I couldn't sound more nerdy if I tried, unless I showed you my variant Spider-Man Todd McFarlane covers one at a time, all professionally rated and every-thing. I mean, what self-respecting seventeen year old starts a damn club? That's some little kid stuff, right? True, and my only saving grace was that I started it when I was still fifteen, which is a little more acceptable.

The Kids of Sick Parents Club (KSPC if you wanna sound cool) was started by me right after my mom's break-down. It was then that I realized, among a lot of other realizations that would come later, that the kids like me, the ones being raised by parents who were less than themselves because of some ailment—whether it was mental illness, or alcoholism, or a medical sickness—we all had a few things in common. I wrote them down in my charter (that's right, there was also a charter).

1: We grew up too damn fast, mostly because we had no choice in the matter of how long we got to hold onto our innocence.

2: We saw and heard things no kid should have to ever see or hear, usually in our own homes, where no one else saw or heard those things but us.

3: We were tough in ways that could never be replicated with any other life experience, a kind of shell that you only get by going through the things we went through.

4: We were sad as hell, but the last thing we wanted was your pity, your 'awws', or your attempt at understanding something you couldn't understand. Mostly we just wanted a break.

So I was the founding member of my club. Really, I was the only member, though I know a lot of you out there are honorary members, even though we never met and I never gave you an official card (I made them, they looked awesome). I knew that I wasn't the only one like me, but I was the only one I knew at the time, at least until I met Annalise, and then the Kids of Sick Parents Club became an organization two strong. We're still growing. As you can tell, I was a little bit of an oddball, but I wore that like a badge. I have no shame in saying that I was an eccentric, artistic, angry, punk rock kid who was a little too into comics for his own good. Maybe that's why Annalise and I found each other, we were fated by the Gods of Weirdness and Dysfunction to meet one day.

Annalise.

Okay, let's pause for a disclaimer: this is the part where I give you the warning to brace yourselves if you want to read any further, buckle your seatbelt, and prepare for some minor turbulence. Some love stories make no sense at all. That's just the way it goes in real life. A lot of things make no sense, if you were to stop and consider their peculiarities, and love most of all. Those strange aspects of love don't make it any less real or impactful, but if you grew up on a steady diet of corny romantic comedies and contrived TV shows, then I can understand your resistance to a lack of convention. We weren't raised to be unconventional, we were raised to believe pop songs should be playing in the background of all our most intimate moments, and that love stories should end with people in love. But that's some movie shit, a diet of falsehoods fed to us like we were animals in a feedlot. Real love is different, it's messy. This is a real love story, so read at your own risk.

Now that we've gotten that out of the way, I have to do my narrator thing and figure out how to encompass Anna's particular flavor of Goddessness in a way that'll make you understand the feeling I had when I looked into her eyes. Well, she wasn't that girl your mom always told you you'd meet one day. If you're a guy you know what I'm talking about, that mythological female your mom had a need to create in her head as your future wife. Maybe she was the daughter of a close family friend, or just some invention of the maternal mind, who knows. That nonexistent, theoretical girl who'd love you unconditionally, make your happiness a priority, give you plenty of attractive babies, that sort of thing. But reality isn't a mother's best wishes, however pure they might be. Reality is an illogical, random series of events guaranteed to mess up all of mom's best laid schemes something awful. Annalise wasn't the ideal girl; she wasn't part of the plan, but she was still perfect to me.

Let's start where it makes sense to start. Yes, she was beautiful. Crazy beautiful. *I-didn't-think-girls-like-you-really-existed* beautiful. Wait, now. That's too common of a compliment, isn't it? Every man says it about the woman he loves, and every woman humbly accepts, not always believing that it's the truth, but loving that he cared enough to say it. In actuality, we aren't specific enough, because there are *types* of beauty, and there are *types* of beautiful. She was the type you read about; the type you see on the big screen but never actually know in person; she was the type of beautiful they meant when the word was invented. They were thinking of Anna, they just didn't realize it.

But let's get past the superficial stuff. What was she like? For one, she was low maintenance, no fancy designer bags or anything like that. She had the kind of frugal practicality that only a poor girl could have; a unique view of material things that makes romance more challenging than advanced calculus, 'cause I couldn't buy her shit without a lecture. I tried to get her flowers this one time—a dozen roses—and she just looked at me like I had lost my damn mind because, well, flowers cost money and then just die, so why bother? *I could buy groceries for the week with the money you spent!* She was wanderlust embodied; fragility in strength's clothing; someone always just barely keeping her inner demons at bay. But she was also really weird and funny at the same time. Check this out.

The girl loved to sleep. She'd sleep in till like 2:30 in the afternoon on weekends, text me good morning, and then take her lazy ass back to sleep! And can you believe that when she'd wake up for real around 3, she had the audacity to tell me she was about to get breakfast. *Are you joking,* I'd ask, *there's no such thing as 3:00 pm breakfast, it just doesn't exist. You, my friend, are about to have lunch, and a fairly late one at that. Lies,* she'd tell me. That was her word, *lies,* she'd say it as a way to tell me she disagreed with whatever I was saying. And boy did she love to disagree with me - I think it might have been her favorite thing to do.

Back to this breakfast thing, though. So I'd reiterate my point cause I was right, and I wasn't about to just let it go. I mean, there's no breakfast at 3:00 pm! You couldn't even make a valid brunch-based argument at that hour. *No, I told her, you're just the girl who slept through the real breakfast, and now had a bad case of the I-Slept-Through-Real-Breakfast-So-I'm-Gonna-Make-Some-Shit-Up blues. You can't just change all the known rules of social behavior in order to accommodate your own laziness. Just accept it; you messed up, start thinking about what you want for lunch. Lies*, she'd repeat. She had this habit of letting me go on short rants to make my point, only to reply with a single word that was intended to transmit that *everything you just said is total crap. You tried it. Get your life* message. *No lies*, I'd continue, *I speak the truth and you just don't wanna admit you lost the argument cause you're competitive, but that doesn't make you right. Well*, she'd say, *I guess it's 8:00 am somewhere, right?*

She was the Catholicist of all Catholic girls (yes, it's a word, I just made it up). Like I said, Peruvian, so I guess there's no small amount of redundancy in calling a good, Spanish girl of any ethnicity a devout Catholic, it kind of comes with the territory. But she went hard. Catholic hard. Like, *don't-use-the-Lord's-name-in-vain* kind of Catholic; like, *my neck will be adorned with a cross at all times* kind of Catholic; like, *no you can't put your hands there, I'm saving myself for marriage* kind of Catholic. That last part was my least favorite one, but I guess that's obvious. For her, Sunday wasn't a day off from work, it was God's day, and I'd get a text only after Sunday prayers with *Mamita* was a wrap. She loved her huge family more than anything. Again, redundant. Spanish girl with a big-ass family. Even without a dad in the house this girl had two sisters, a mom, and about forty cousins. All the damn cousins!

I always got them confused when she told stories about her extended family. Probably because she began each story referring to each and every one of them as *my cousin so-and-so. Who*, I'd ask. My cousin, so-and-so, you know, the one with the Hispanic name that sounds like the other Hispanic names. *Oh, right, them!* I never got them all straight. But it was confusing by sheer numbers alone, which were extreme by non-Hispanic standards. And to make things next-level confusing, the older cousins she was close to she'd refer to as her uncles, even though they weren't. Every time I dared call her out on her complete lack of genealogical understanding (*they're your cousins, you can't just call them by another title because you feel like it*) she'd flip out and threaten to stop talking to me until I called them her uncles. Fine, I said, they're your uncles, not your cousins, how dare I ever say otherwise. Girl literally made me say uncle.

But bizarre family trees aside, family always came first for Anna. She lived with her two half-sisters and her mom in a small basement apartment that they rented, in a part of town that you could have accurately referred to as the wrong side of the tracks. Her oldest sister was about a high school career older than Anna, and the little one was just about to turn double-digits at the time our story begins. I didn't really know either of them because Anna never let me in her apartment, but I'll save that for later. But I knew that each of the girls had a different dad, none of whom were around, and that their mom was a Peruvian immigrant who understood more English then she ever let on, but spoke almost none.

Annalise taught me more than I can fit in these pages, and maybe I did the same for her, but more than anything she taught me about hope, even when she had none herself, and she taught me about forgiveness even when she couldn't muster any for those around her. *Hope is for suckers*, she'd tell me, *and nothing good happens without something bad happening, too. It's fine*, she'd say when I tried to comfort her,

I'm used to it, I'll live. Mom used to say the same sometimes. *I'm okay, baby, don't worry about me.*

Mom. She's as much a part of my story as Annalise is, but the complex truth is that they're intertwined in a way that gets hard to separate logically, like when you put your keys and your headphones in the same pocket and try to pull just one of them out. Doesn't work. Their stories are stuck together, glued only by the impact each had on me a long time ago.

Brace yourself for an elastic metaphor. I call it elastic 'cause I'm gonna stretch it out, like Plastic Man used to stretch his arms to save people who were in trouble. It won't break, I promise. There are people who migrate through our lives like the background characters in a mediocre movie; the B actors of life who live on in freeze-framed memories, but who don't really matter in any way that you can conceive the word *matter* to mean. But then there are the ones who are cast in the important roles; the roles that matter and forever alter the narrative, and upend the lives we know, leaving our existence forever altered. We only get a few of these people, no matter how long we live, and Annalise was one of mine, she was *the* one. Loving Anna didn't make me, but it may have saved me, and that's a story that needs telling, so here it is.

My book. My love letter. Our Story.

Interlude

WHERE WE PAUSE THE NARRATIVE FOR ME TO TELL
YOU ALL ABOUT THAT MOST INSIDIOUS OF SOUL-
KILLERS.

The *Bleh* was a force, a darkness without end, an event horizon.

It occupied an unknown quantity of space, or perhaps it was space itself, a deformed version of it anyhow, into which those diverse emotions we called happiness went to disappear. Where they went was anyone's guess, but it was clear that their purest forms were never to be observed again. Maybe the *Bleh* was a wormhole, the other end of which produced the bastards of our happiness.

Although the nature of its origins remained unknown, it was, without question, a family thing. It was an inheritance, a thing passed down through generations like some shitty heirloom nobody wanted, but got in their grandma's will nonetheless. Or maybe it was biological, its characteristics woven into the very fabric of our DNA. Or then again, maybe it was an environmental thing, our genetic expression gone mad, influenced by the most random of things outside of our control. It was probably all the above.

As far as I could trace back with my amateur genealogical skills, which were highly suspect, the *Bleh* first expressed itself in the new world, a gift from my great grandfather. That dude lost his mind and nearly killed his whole family one morning over coffee and danish to resolve some ridiculous issues that are lost to history. His family didn't fall under his knife, but the *Bleh* jumped from him (or perhaps it multiplied, who knows) to his children— all of them—four siblings who'd each have it manifest somewhat differently. My great uncle similarly lost his mind, though his *Bleh* made him suicidal instead of homicidal; my other great uncle was just weird, a hermit who no one ever spoke to, which was probably just fine with him. My great aunt never married, which didn't fundamentally make her crazy, but the reason for the lack of a marriage was her propensity towards strangeness ranging in intensity from 'a little eccentric' to 'that strange lady who wanders the neighborhood late at night'.

Now my grandmother was another story altogether. Her expression of the *Bleh* was on some next level. Hers transcended the general strangeness imparted to her siblings, and instead she became just like her abusive father; someone capable and willing to spread the *Bleh* to others. Enter my mom. The *Bleh* was passed onto her through the damn umbilical cord, right into the bloodstream. It lied dormant for a little while, but even by the age of ten that shit was playing games with her, convincing her she didn't wanna live anymore and making her depressed before she was old enough to even spell the word. Like many forces in this world, it goes by different names, most of them too imprecise and vague to have much meaning, depending on who you ask: mental illness, a chemical imbalance, just plain crazy. A beast with many heads. A force with many names. But its lack of a proper name doesn't make it any less real.

What about me, you ask? I had it too. No doubt it lived inside of me. How could it not? It was my inheritance after all. But I was a fighter like my Mom, who never met a *Bleh* she couldn't scrap with. That was also my inheritance. That was the strange part. I was the inheritor of both my destruction and my salvation; it was only a matter of which one got to me first.

TWO

Where I realize that even when thrown by
my best friend with the noblest of
intentions, a french fry in the face is still
really annoying.

Our Story begins in a typical, all American high school
which sat only a few blocks from my house. I'd gone to
Catholic school for 9th and 10th grades, but after my
parents finally realized the error of their ways in sending
me there I ended up at the local high school. You
remember the type; a large, box-shaped building crammed
with angry, lonely, and silly adolescents. That place where
the day started too early and ended too late, and where we
came to follow rules for a living.

That was the world I lived in when I met Annalise, the
building where kids spent the most formative years of their
lives; that strange dramaturgy where we pretended to be
who we thought we were. It was a stage, where the daily
dramas of breakups, failed tests, and personal problems got
played out for huge, unwanted audiences to see, judge, and
leave a review on Yelp. And occasionally we learned stuff,
too. I hated high school. We just never got along; one of
those toxic relationships you hear self-help authors talking
about on daytime TV talk shows. We were bad for one

another. Abusive, no good enablers of the very worst qualities in each other.

Sixteenth century bell schedules.

Notes copied off blackboards into marble notebooks.

One more year of my life to get thoroughly zombified.

On one of those momentous occasions when a teacher taught me something, I remember my World History teacher telling us about The Encounter; the first time that Europeans landed their blue-eyes on the shores of the Americas (and we all know how well things went from there). The name stuck with me. Two worlds colliding, meeting for the first time, and each changing the other forever. Well, Annalise and I had our own Encounter, and it happened on a Monday.

It was a wear-your-hood-in-school kind of day. But then again, what day wasn't? That morning my homeroom teacher called me Emo because of said hood, but that was just the kind of things teachers said when they needed to classify you. *You see us as you want to see us. In the simplest terms, the most convenient definitions.* I'd been called Emo more than once at school, but I guess I was too Emo to care what adults called me. It was a normal first day of the week, unspectacular except for what eventually happened, and for the fact that I was about to get ruthlessly pegged in the face by my so-called best friend. The sensations of hard, hot, and wet all hit my cheek at the exact same time. "Did you just throw a fry at me?" I couldn't believe I had to ask such a thing, but I was pretty sure that's what had just happened.

"Yeah, so?"

"So?" I asked. "What the hell? And it's a greasy one, too."

"That's what bothered you about it? So, like, if it had

been a little drier you'd be cool with it bouncing off your cheek?"

"No, I wouldn't," I declared angrily. "But it would have been less offensive."

"I didn't mean to offend," my soon to be ex- best friend said back to me. "I meant to get you out of la la land. Wake up, man."

"I was day dreaming of happier things," I told him. "Sure as hell better than this place."

"Logan, an impoverished African nation in the middle of armed rebellion is better than this place. When did you become so obvious?"

"About the same time you decided it was cool to throw your lunch at my face to get my attention. A tap on the shoulder would have worked just fine."

"So what were you fantasizing about? No, wait, dumb question. So is today *the* day?"

The day he was referring to was the one where I actually grew a set and talked to Annalise. And yes, I'd decided that it was, in fact, *the* day. I'd tortured myself for an entire year over this issue. That's a full twelve months of self-induced frustration, and romantic comedy-like pining from a distance. I'd decided that it was finally time to act.

"Yeah, it is." Before I was done with my affirmation another fry hit me. "Shit, what was that one for?"

"For lying. You're a terrible liar."

I spent a year telling myself that every upcoming day was *the* day, the talking-to-Annalise day; mark it on your calendar. I'd say it before bed, as though sleep would make it a reality when I woke up, like those fools who try to learn a language when they're unconscious. I'd made the false declaration of speaking to her so many times that I didn't even believe myself any more. Apparently Pete didn't either. Maybe I was a terrible liar.

27

"Thank you, I guess."

"It wasn't a compliment."

"Wait, so being a good liar is the goal?"

"Don't try to confuse me," he said back. "There's only one goal, and so far you haven't come close to accomplishing it." He was right, of course, but it wasn't my fault. That's just what girls as stunning as Annalise did, they made you hesitate.

So enter Pete, the best of the friends I ever made, if you needed a title, but if I was being polygraph-honest with you, he was my only real friend. I had acquaintances, sure, and kids I was cool with at school, but the word friend meant something to me, and Pete was the only one who fit that criteria. We went way back, farther than most friends in high school went, to a kindergarten class of long ago, where we bonded over a shared package of Fig Newtons my mom packed for my snack, and our mutual hatred of our Megabitch of a teacher, Ms. Maron.

Now, when I call her a Megabitch I do so for a reason. The woman was pure evil; sent from some yet undiscovered level of Hell that even Dante would've struggled to articulate properly. She was a panic attack generator; the kind of teacher that sowed the seeds of hating school nice and early. Everything made her angry. It was like she woke up each morning just barely suppressing the urge to murder someone, and then drove to work to teach five year olds how to color and count things. She existed in a near constant state of irritation, and when she had dominion over our five year old lives, she was nothing short of the type of evil you imagined lived under your bed when mom and dad shut off your nightlight and left the room.

My general weirdness and misanthropy came later in my life, but I was a pretty normal little kid. I was prone to intense contemplation and scowls that made me look way too serious for my age, but still, pretty normal. I was nice, polite, and I smiled. This got me automatically pegged as the good one, and Pete, with his penchant for disregarding authority, got labeled the troublemaker. This perception followed us throughout our childhood and adolescence, haunting Pete with an unfounded reputation for all things rude and disrespectful, the kind of rep that gossipy teachers (which, let's face it, is all of them) just loved to internalize. Pete was ruined at five, condemned to mostly unfounded stereotypes that would shape his self-perception and behavior for years, and for what? Who even remembers? Kid probably asked for another serving of fruit punch or some inane shit that was enough to set that crazy woman off.

And what really made our friendship work was the balance between our personalities. In some ways we were simpatico, blood brothers. But our temperaments were North and South poles. Whereas I was overly analytical, Pete was uncomplicated in ways that just made our friendship work. Take this Annalise thing. While my overly serious self was contemplating all the different outcomes of approaching Annalise, weighing the pros and cons and formulating elaborate strategies, Pete was more of the *screw it, just walk up and start talking to her* mindset. Since middle school he'd always been the one talking to the girl while other guys were too afraid to do much but stare like creeps. A side note is appropriate here: not being creepy when you're secretly in love with a girl is harder to accomplish than it may sound. Trust me, whether you've ever stopped to take a selfie in this state or not, when you're in the midst of some intense contemplation about a particular girl, best to not look directly at her for too long. There's just no way yet invented to not look like a stalker who's contemplating the most efficient kidnapping technique to employ.

"The goal is within reach, my friend, just you wait and see."

"That's exactly what I'll do," Pete said. "I'll wait until I see it with my own eyes to believe it."

Full disclosure here, at that point in my life I had a virtually non-existent relationship with all female creatures who didn't give birth to me. There were girls I liked over the years, but I lacked the vocabulary and requisite bravery to ever approach them properly. I became one of those borderline creepy, admire-you-from-afar kind of dudes, ever the true romantic, but always without the actual girl to apply those sentiments to. This worked for me at first, but then the other guys around me started to lap me in the girl department.

For example, a bunch of the guys at my old Catholic school used to make weekly pilgrimages to meet girls at our sister school, the all-girls *Our Lady of Whatever-the-Hell*, but I never went with them. I got invited a few times, but it was never my thing. Like true trackers, those boys just knew how to hunt; they knew the geography, the social behavior of their prey, how to isolate the girls with morals from the rest of the pack for an easier kill, all that. Sometimes they'd come back with a trophy, and other times they'd return with stories of how they just barely missed, and how next time they'd bag one for sure. I wouldn't have been surprised to have seen one of the seniors driving around with a Catholic school girl tied to his bumper, plaid skirt and all. I'm not saying I would have rejected a plaid wearing Catholic school girl had one serendipitously appeared in front of me and started a conversation about Spider-Man, but that shit didn't happen outside of a really bad movie, so my first few high school years were lonely ones indeed.

"Look, man, you're overthinking this. How do you think I met Lindsey? I went up to her and started saying shit, any shit. To be honest, I don't even remember what I said. She probably does 'cause girls remember that stuff, but the point is that it worked. I was just myself, and I started talking. There's not much else to it." This was the truth. Pete was like that, the perfect best friend extrovert to my painfully introverted self.

"Yeah, that's not me. You know this. I was the same when we were five. Nothing's changed. The idea of it just gives me anxiety."

"Don't mention the kindergarten year. I'm still scared by she-who-must-not-be-named."

"I know."

"But back to this Annalise thing, you know what they say?" *The Council of They.* Pete was a card-carrying member.

"No," I joked. "Tell me what they say?"

"He who hesitates doesn't get the shit he wants."

"I'm pretty sure you're misquoting there, but I get it."

"You're going to spend your last year doing this, talking and analyzing everything to death while some other guy goes and scoops her up. Then what?" The truth in Pete's words hit me with a force harder than any fry could generate.

"Is that how you got Lindsey? You scooped?"

"I'm a master scooper," he joked. "And look at Lindsey, she's hot. You don't think there were guys like you wanting to talk to her who just never had the courage to? Of course there were. I'm not special, man, I just took my shot."

"Don't tell Lin Manuel, but I think I might be throwing mine away. I guess the power of that song was lost on me."

I had seen Annalise around, here and there, in the summer before our junior year. Girl radiated energy, expelled the essence of life from her pores. Even before I ever spoke a word to her; before emails were exchanged and rocks visited, and everything that followed, it was her energy that I fell in love with. You probably still have no idea what I mean, do you? Alright, let's put it like this: guys gave off energies that invoked questions, and girls had energies that represented answers. Everyone had their own charge, and all most of us were really looking for was the person with the complimentary charge. We might as well have been walking around with plus or minus signs tattooed on our foreheads. Anna's energy spoke to me, and since the first time I laid eyes on her I knew that she was the girl of my dreams.

"She's right there," Pete said, pointing at the other end of the cafeteria. "And you're gonna stay here with me, getting hit in the face with more fries? Consider your life choices right now."

"I'm telling you, man, today's the day. I feel it in my bones."

"What I feel is the weight of your skinny ass at this table. What I should feel is you popping up, going over there, and saying hi to her."

I didn't have much experience with girls, but I noticed by watching other guys that experience didn't really matter when it came to the approaching phase. Once you were on the inside, experience mattered in a relationship, but I'd seen braver dudes than I go down by rattling off a Gatling-gun barrage of bad lines towards the wrong girl.

One guy, this kid Michael, used to hang around with Pete and I like one of those sucker-fish that attach themselves to the bottom of the tank and never let go. Couldn't get rid of him. Nothing worked. Being the level headed one of our dynamic duo I would always attempt the polite resolution. *Look, Mike, I'm not sure this friendship is a good fit, we're into different things, plus Pete and I have known each other since we survived that Megabitch in kindergarten, and you know how it is —bonding of shared trauma and all—so maybe you should go hang out with those kids over there.* Break up game strong. Didn't work worth a damn, though. Kid couldn't take the hint. *Oh, okay, I understand,* he'd say, and then he'd show up, tray of food in hand, at our lunch table the next day.

So anyhow, one day when our stage five clinger of a friend didn't bother to sit with us, Pete and I looked around and watched this fool actually approach a girl. Not just any girl, mind you, but one of the top 5 hottest in the school. Now she was no Annalise, mind you, but Jacklyn Arriata was not to be taken lightly. She was a formidable enemy who'd vanquished many adolescent boy's hopes and dreams when they got lured in by her face, not realizing that she listed her home town as *Sirenum Scopuli* on all official documents. By the time our fake friend walked up to her he was already done, he just didn't know it yet. He was like one of those old Looney Tunes episodes where the Coyote ran off the cliff while chasing the Road Runner, only there was a five second delay before he realized that there was no more ground beneath him.

From the outside it looked like a friendly enough exchange, but that's only because you had to have a trained eye in what disasters looked like when they didn't look like disasters to everyone. I didn't know much about girls, but I knew a disaster when I saw one. I couldn't actually hear the words exchanged between them, but it was one of those situations where even the most socially illiterate person could have interpreted the body language. It started promising enough. Michael looked like a kid on Christmas morning, all doughy-eyed and excited. Fool thought he had a chance. I guess ignorance really was bliss, but that senti-ment didn't last more than a sentence or two. She started cackling; not laughing, straight cackling. Head leaned back, mouth open like a crocodile about to make quick work of some small animal. The sounds of her cackle made everyone in the cafeteria stare at the whole event like people stare at a car wreck on the side of the road; with some weird mix of fascination and horror. Never saw Michael mess with any girls again after that slaying.

Now I'm not saying I was worried that Annalise would treat me like poor Michael got treated, but seeing things like that didn't help my confidence any. There were other extinction events when it came to boy/girl interactions that also gave me pause. My friend Selena—who I only call a friend in the most passive of senses—was that person who I was close to when we were kids but we just kind of drifted apart. She showed up at my house one day after school, tears in her eyes, face all red and blotchy. *What's wrong*, I asked her, *are you ok. No*, she said, *he broke my heart*. The "He" in question was Albert Dessio, who everyone called Alby.

I could have told Selena that this was gonna happen, anyone who knew Alby could have (the dude's track record with girls was legendary) but try telling some love-struck sixteen year old girl that she's making the wrong life choices with the guys in her life. Good luck with that. So she showed up at my house looking like she'd just gone twelve hard rounds with Life and lost, sobbing in that dramatic way where you can barely talk 'cause you're hyperventilating. *Calm down*, I said. *Come in, we can talk*. She told me how Alby was seeing other girls (no secret there), how he was verbally abusive (anyone with ears could hear this) and how her family never liked him (good for you Mom and Dad). I listened and we talked for a little while, until she was calm enough to head back home, probably to get back together with Alby, despite all evidence that it was a terrible idea, but before she left she asked me something that I still remember like it was yesterday.

"Do boys even cry when stuff like this happens?"

"Some," I said to her, handing her a tissue from one of the many boxes around my house. "Some do. But usually not the types of boys who girls go for to begin with."

As I was remembering that another fry hit me in the face. "Alright, for real, stop throwing your lunch in my face before I beat your ass."

"If only you could be this brave all of the time, you might actually have something to do on the weekend. . ." Pete stopped in mid-sentence retort, and I didn't even need to look at him to know the look of complete embarrassment on his face. It was the kind of expression that the muscles in your face are just forced to make after you've said something so profoundly stupid that there's no other appropriate response. "I'm sorry, man," he said apologetically. "Forget I said anything. I didn't mean—"

"I know, man, don't apologize. I wish I could forget sometimes too." I stopped him from apologizing further.

"So how's Mom doing, anyway?" I loved Pete like a brother, hell, he was my brother for all intents and purposes, but I hated that question, however well intended. I guess what annoyed me the most about it was that I was never sold on the idea that whoever asked me that question wanted a real answer. They asked for different reasons of their own: to be nice, to feel like they're being nice even if they didn't care, some sense of social obligation, or, in Pete's case, as an antidote for the foot lodged in his mouth. Regardless of their motivation I never felt like any of it had to do with her, with Mom, because if I answered them honestly I'd ruin their day; I'd make them cry, or at the least just end the conversation with their mood thoroughly ruined, and who wanted that? So to avoid the awkward-ness, I just compiled some rehearsed answers, delivered in perfect rhythm.

Fine. She's fine. A little better, thanks for asking. Yeah, good days and bad days, you know, but she's a fighter. My soul left my body when I had to say that stuff, but sometimes I needed to protect people from the truth they thought they wanted but really didn't. I had to protect everyone. So my patented move after delivering one of my expressions was to change the subject, which never got any resistance from whoever I was talking to. They had done their socially obligated duty, now it was on to much appreciated inane chit-chat. Pete was smart enough to take the hint.

"Well, Annalise is gone. Good job."

"Do you think your ridicule helps? It doesn't. It just makes me feel like shit."

"That's on you. I'm just pointing out the truth. But you know it's all from a place of love, right? Literally nothing would make me as happy as to see you two going to prom. I'm just frustrated."

"Imagine how I feel. But I know, thank you. I appre-ciate it. And she's not gone, she's just waiting for me in my next class, remember?"

"Right," he said. "Psychology."

"Psychology," I repeated, a smile creeping over my face. "I don't even need the credits, I have enough to grad-uate, and Mr. A's a goon. There's only one reason to go to Psychology." Pete rolled his eyes because he knew what I was referring to. The high school scheduling gods bestowed the bounty of putting my Peruvian goddess in the same senior elective as me, which kind of made not talking to her even more unacceptable. I had her in the same room every day but I hadn't acted. As far as Psychology went, I didn't much care that the class was taught terribly, or that I already knew most of the curriculum from just reading books on my own. That was all incidental. The only thing that mattered was that she was there, and all I had to do was take my chance. Easier said than done.

Besides the intimidation of her face alone, I couldn't really tell you why I was so paralyzed when it came to interacting with her; all indications pointed to her being super friendly. She was the rarest of high school types: the cool, friendly, hot girl who didn't realize the extent to which she was any of those things. In high school, encountering girls like her was like seeing a Yeti in the woods of Montana: no one believed that shit even existed, and if you told your friends you had seen one they'd tell you that you were crazy.

After lunch Pete and I walked to Psychology. As Mr. A was beginning his lesson on god-knows-what, I remembered that I had selectively forgotten that the class was doing group projects. Just in case you don't remember high school so clearly, 'group projects' is teacher-code for *I don't wanna teach today, I want to wander the room like a nomad and look over people's shoulders in a feeble attempt to look like I'm teaching, should the Principal walk by the classroom*. I didn't even care anymore, and at that point I'd lost the will to do anything except graduate.

Mr. A started passing out the instructions for our projects to the first kid in each row, and I waited like a good soldier for the three kids in front of me to pass back the work. On the projector he had our group assignments, topics, and members. I glanced up from my phone in distain, expecting the standard teacher groupings; me with a bunch of dumb kids who don't care about anything, and expect me to do all of the work. (*Mr. A teaches Psychology, hadn't he ever heard of the Ringleman Effect?*) Situations like that showed how paradoxical being labeled 'the smart kid' could be. In school that label didn't necessarily mean praise or accolades, it mostly meant that you did the lazy and stupid kids' work for them. Within the established high school taxonomy, my tribe's village had been invaded and we'd all been taken as forced labor for the intellectually inferior Stupid & Lazy tribes, who had formed an unstoppable alliance years ago, before written record existed.

But when I looked at the screen I couldn't believe my eyes. The PowerPoint slide read:

GROUP 1: Logan, Annalise, Jacob, Samantha (Topic: mental illness)

My elation was quickly replaced with a unique sort of terror that got my heart racing in my chest like the physiological precursor to a panic attack. I realized that I was also holding my breath, and that passing out on the floor in front of Annalise's desk would've been a bad look, and probably damaged my chances with her some, so I took a few deep breaths to relax myself. The kid in front of me passed me the instructions, and I took them mindlessly from him. Samantha and Jacob had to get up and walk across the room to sit with us, since our desks were already in a sort of group. I waved them over to politely indicate that I wasn't moving an inch. I turned and passed the instructions to Annalise, and she smiled at me. "Thanks," she said. "I hate group work, no offense."

"Me, too," I told her. "We'll get through it together, alright?"

"Sounds like a plan."

I turned my desk around to face her, and I tried my best not to go into creep mode, but she was so damn beautiful that it was hard not to. Instead I looked down and we read the instructions for our dumb project in silence.

"So it says we need to exchange contact information. Here's my email and cell, okay?" She leaned over and started writing in my binder, and it was surreal. I was so excited about being in a group with her that I forgot that we were only half of the group, we were still waiting for the other two to walk over. Jacob and Samantha. Never had there been two more incidental space fillers in human form. I hesitate to even give them any space in our narrative, but the rest of what happened that day wouldn't make any sense without them, so here they appear for the first and last time, the alpha and omega of useless characters.

Samantha was nice enough as people went, but dumber than the decision her dad made to not wear a condom. But dumb was easy enough to navigate. Jacob was another matter altogether. I knew the kid passively from elementary school and around the neighborhood. He was *that* kid. Like how the law of educational averages dictates that there must always be at least one completely hopeless, irretrievable asshole in any group of thirty kids, and Jacob was always happy to play the part. Teachers hated but tolerated him, I suspected mostly out of some sense of professionalism coupled with their pay checks. I'm sure if he was their age any one of the male teachers in the building would have beaten Jacob half to death outside of a bar for saying something insulting to their wife or girlfriend. But as the universe had it they were tasked with educating young Jacob.

Personally, I had nothing against the kid except for his archetypal douche-baggery. He was loud, generally obnoxious (those two qualities were always like peanut butter and chocolate for assholes), ignorant, and needlessly insulting to almost everyone he spoke to. But before that day my hatred of him was philosophical, we'd never had a problem with one another. I always avoided people like Jacob, but the social engineering of school forced people who would otherwise stay away from one another into increasingly smaller and more intimate groups. Then again, it also forced me into a group with Annalise. The universe had balance.

"What's our topic?" Jacob asked in a voice that was way too loud. Samantha, our group's resident idiot, offered an answer.

"Mental illness, it's on the handout."

"Oh yeah, so we get to do a project on crazy people, that's awesome."

"Yeah, not really, Jacob," I interjected. "There's a little more to it than that. Plus, crazy is a dumb word, most people with mental issues aren't crazy, that's ignorant." I couldn't hold back with people like Jacob, which is why I put a lot of energy into carefully avoiding him. I almost didn't blame him; he seemed genetically programed to say dumb shit at the wrong time.

"Screw you, man, I'm not ignorant!" He didn't know when to stop; didn't even know that he needed to stop, and I felt my blood start to boil. "And, by the way, yeah they are. If you need pills and doctors to not slit your wrists or be a complete mess, you're a crazy person, I'm sorry."

He wasn't actually sorry, but he became so after I jumped out of my seat and tackled him out of his desk and onto to the floor for the beating my already balled fists seemed determined to give him. We were on the floor within seconds, and I wrapped around him like a vice, as he became the unwilling recipient of years of grappling I had done with my dad. Though it was hard to perceive those things accurately when you were in the middle of them, I'm pretty sure I got off at least three clean shots and a few on his arm before I felt a pair of large adult hands wrap around my waist, and pull me up onto my feet.

It was Mr. A, and he wasn't pleased. Even though he coached varsity boy's football, and no doubt dealt with some rough physical situations, this type of thing was different. This was Navy-SEAL style, close quarter combat. I'm sure that situation is the exact type that teachers dread: it's like every fear about the barbaric nature of teenagers laid bare, as we literally tried to kill one another like apes, and poor Mr. A had to put his advanced degrees to work to pull us apart. He threw me aside and pushed through the apathetic crowd of my classmates to attend to Jacob, who had a visibly bloody nose. He looked embarrassed and kind of sad, but that was the price of stupidity.

I wished that I could have beaten the ignorance completely out of him, that it would have leaked out of his body, and pooled on the linoleum floor as his blood was doing at that moment, but of course that isn't what happened. I just got to beat on a stupid person for a few seconds, which nonetheless offered its own real, if fleeting, sense of satisfaction. Mr. A yelled at me to go to the Dean's office on the main floor, and I obliged without protest because, despite having a temper, I was a pretty respectful kid.

High school deans were bullshit; the personification of self-important pseudo-authority, with their ridiculous color-coded disciplinary cards and unchecked powers. What almighty school principal, in all their vast wisdom, decided to grant a handful of already incompetent teachers even more power by making them the fake judges of a school building? As I sat there waiting on the mercy of this random math teacher who got paid an extra few hundred dollars to pass sentence on troubled kids, in he walked. In the classroom Mr. Longo wasn't so bad; I had him for geometry when I first came to the school in junior year. But context is everything, the real determinant of people's behavior, and in that shitty little office Mr. Longo was king, a complete and utter power-happy prick.

"Mr. Santiagooo," he said, dragging out the vowels in my name for dramatic effect. I didn't like his tone at all, or the air of arrogance in his demeanor. It amazed me how power changed people. In the classroom Mr. Longo was the lamb, at the mercy of a room full of 30 tired, angry 16-year-olds who gave no shits about discreet math or geometry. In that office, with that title, Mr. Longo decided to exact his revenge on petty high school criminals to the full extent of his power.

"Got into a fight, did you? Is that right?" The pretense was that there was an actual discussion to be had, which there wasn't. He was playing the role of interrogator, probably modeled after some cop show he watched late at night, alone and sad in his little basement apartment. In this fantasy gone insane he was the clever investigator who already knew the answers to the questions he asked the perp. I wanted to complete his fantasy by being a total dick, and telling him that by all standard definitions, what happened in Mr. A's Psych class fell more appropriately under the category of a 'beating' than it did a 'fight', but I held back and allowed him to hand down his ruling uninterrupted.

"So, Mr. Santiago, tomorrow, you're going to in-school suspension periods 1-6, I'll have your teachers send work for you to do, and if you're late, or if you skip any periods you'll have it again the following day also, are we clear?" The last line he heard in a movie, for sure. It sounded authoritative because he knew that I'd have to say 'yes', which I did. Then I got dismissed to go back to class.

As I walked to my next period I managed to see Pete

through the sea of humanity that filled the hallways. He didn't take physics, but in the classroom next to mine he had another one of the stupid electives he managed to pack his senior schedule with. The wall in between the two classrooms was something of a tribal meeting ground, a place where we gathered each day to talk and make plans.

"So what happened?"

"What do you think? Standard Dean bs"

"ISS?"

I nodded. "So I'm getting out of here, I can't anymore…" I trailed off, lost in angry thoughts. I never cut class, but I just couldn't stomach another two periods of notes and lectures. Pete didn't argue with me, he saw the resolve in my face. "Text me later on, alright?" I walked out the side door of the school and tried to discreetly head for the street without making eye contact with any adults. I lived close to the school, so it was a quick walk home. A few blocks later I was there, an hour and a half early from the time I normally got home, but Mom didn't notice. She didn't notice much of anything by that point in her life. It was a terrible thought to have, but I didn't want to deal with her either. I walked past her and up to my room, where I got some much needed sleep.

I woke up to the feeling of vibration in my pocket, not realizing how much time had passed. When I came to my senses I figured that it must have been Pete, texting me like I asked him to earlier, though I still wasn't in any mood to talk. When I unlocked my phone I saw that it wasn't a text at all, it was an email. And not just any email, it was an email from *her*. I closed my bedroom door and immediately took a screen shot. I wanted to record this for posterity so that one day, when I was a decrepit old man sitting around an old age home, I would be able to wow the other geezers with tales of the day Annalise had emailed me. I opened it up immediately.

So I know this has nothing to do with Psychology. . .well, sort of, in a weird way. I mean, not Psychology class. . .I don't even know what I'm saying or why I'm bothering you with this. I know we've never even talked before and you don't give a shit about what I'm writing, but I needed to tell someone. I'm done with school and I think I'm gonna drop out. That's all.

-Annalise

The email was time-stamped a half hour before. Almost out of instinct, without much forethought, I hit reply and started pecking away at my keyboard.

Hey...it's Logan. I've just got this, sorry. Umm...you shouldn't drop out. I know that sounds weird coming from the kid who hates school and just got into a lot of trouble, but you shouldn't drop out. We're seniors and have less than a year left.

As I hit 'send' I realized what a terrible reply I had just offered to someone who was clearly in crisis and needed someone to listen to her. I also thought that I had waited a year to talk to this girl, and I when I finally got the opportunity I had nearly beaten a kid unconscious in front of her. If she was really serious about dropping out of school that email wasn't going to do much to change her mind. Right then my phone vibrated again. That couldn't have been her, I thought, it had only been like a minute since I sent my reply, maybe less, actually. I unlocked my phone again.

Hey – thank you for listening. I still think I'm dropping out but thanks. See you tomorrow in Psych.

-Annalise

I started typing back right away. The universe had granted me a second chance at talking to her, and there would be no more awkward rambling, so I began email number four:

So, listen, I really, really don't think that you should drop out. Like, I think it's a bad idea. My mom dropped out of college. I know that's not the same thing, but it sort of is, and she always wished she hadn't, even years later she still talks about it. I don't know...I just think that you're too smart to drop out, and I wouldn't want you to regret it later on. I know I don't even know you like that, but I just have some experience with this, and I think that you're strong enough to ride out the last year; it's only a couple of months. I'll help you...I don't even know what that means, exactly, but I will – anything you need. If you need to talk, or whatever. Don't drop out, or at least consider not.

-Logan

I hit send and my heart started racing furiously. I wasn't exactly clear why my words induced panic, maybe because I hoped that they would have some sort of impact on her decision. I put my phone down and tried to get some homework done. As I did, I realized that at some point high school teachers just decided to give way too many projects to their seniors: a project on political parties for Participation and Government; a project on product marketing for Economics; even the then-doomed Psychology project on mental illness. As I sat there, drowning in instruction packets and grading rubrics, I believed very strongly that I would never use PowerPoint this much again in my entire life. I actually missed tests.

About a half hour into making up my Econ slideshow my phone shook the bed. I knew that it was her at that point, and I felt like we were texting each other, even though it was only a rapid-fire email chain. Or maybe I just wanted to be texting her so badly that I pretended one was like the other. I didn't care either way, all I knew was that I was about to have my fifth line of dialogue with Annalise. Call it whatever you want, I couldn't read it fast enough.

Wow umm I'm very touched that you took time out of your day to write this email to me. It's not that I hate school or I think I don't have enough potential to finish it because I know I do. It's just hard when you have a lot on your plate. . It's hard to stay focused in school when you have problems like the ones I have...I'm not going into detail because I'm sure it would be irrelevant to you (not to be said in a bad way, because no one really cares) and no it's not relationship problems that's childish. But thankyou for sending me your email, it truly made me open my eyes to why it's not the best decision to make. And btw, what happened after Mr. A threw you out?

-Anna

I stared at my screen without moving for a few minutes, probably longer than someone should stare at their screen without moving. Had someone been observing, I probably looked like I was having a stroke and my body had merely forgotten to fall, lifeless, to the ground. While in mid-fake-stroke, I made a few observations about the entire exchange: (1) she wrote thank you as one word and I couldn't figure out why, (2) She called herself 'Anna', and (3) I touched her? *Holy shitballs*, I thought my I was just rambling on and on, but I guess…I touched her, wow, and (4) I needed to write back. And so I did:

So after Mr. A threw me out I went to the dean and got ISS for tomorrow. Such bullshit, but what can I do? Anyways, I'm glad I could help, does that mean you're not gonna drop out? Or at least that you're considering not? I hope so. And I get it if you don't wanna talk about whatever problems you referred to in your email, but I promise you that it's not irrelevant. The reason I got heated today in class was because that topic hits home for me, literally. My mom, she's…sick. I don't talk about it a lot but it's hard and I help take care of her, so I get it. If you ever wanna talk about it, I'm a good listener.

-Logan

I realized that I had just let Annalise into a secret part of my life. I didn't tell anyone about mom. Pete was the only one who really knew what was going on, and that was because he was a brother to me. When we were little he used to call my mom 'Mom', and he spent most of his afternoons and weekends at my house, getting a second upbringing, meals and motherly advice included. My bed vibrated again, and the sound shocked me out of my own head. It was Annalise.

I honestly didn't expect you to share more about your personal life. Not that I don't care, but I for one can't open up like that because I would regret it immediately for some reason. My personal life is similar to the one you have shared with me but only to a certain degree. Add that with mental problems I have myself. I don't want you to think less of me because of my mental issues, which is why I don't openly share it, but I

think it's somewhat fair since you've shared yours. However, I do want you to know that though it might not seem like it, I am truly trying my best to keep everything sane around me (school wise, home wise, mentally wise). I can see why dropping out isn't the best solution for my problems, which is why I am finishing high school and hoping to graduate in time. I just assumed you would be like "oh no, what have I gotten myself into?" I don't know how this escalated to me emailing you this, but it helped me in a way and I wanted to say thankyou. And that sucks about ISS. We should cut school tomorrow, just saying. It'll help me fight my *Bleh*.

-Anna

I made a second set of observations: (1) I needed to ask her about the 'thank you' thing, it was bothering me, but it was really cute at the same time and I never wanted her to write it any other way, (2) how was this actually happening right now (less an observation than question, but whatever), (3) she's opened up to me a lot in a few emails, what does that mean (another question), (4) What the hell was a *Bleh*?, and (5) She wanted to hang out??? I read that last line about twenty seven times, each time I believed it just a little bit more, yet I still didn't entirely believe it at all. Of all voices to hear at that moment I heard Mr. Longo, warning me in his best authoritative teacher voice what would happen if I skipped out on my punishment tomorrow. Then I remembered that both he and his punishments were idiotic; and that I would have gladly spent a decade of my life in a maximum security cell with a criminally insane cell-mate for the chance to hang out with Annalise. I wrote back quickly, and after that our average email turnaround time to each other was about 60 seconds, until I suggested that we just text one another because, well, we basically were already.

Me: Hey…oh my god, yeah, I'd love to. But what are we gonna do?

Annalise: I don't know… I'll go wherever, so looks like we just need a plan then... You're putting me in a difficult position to decide where we should go... I was about to say we can get cookies from McDonald's. Those cheer me up for some weird reason.

Me: You wanna go to McDonald's?

Annalise: Not really, I just want McDonald's cookies – they make me happy.

Me: I've never had cookies from McDonald's – I'm more of a coffee guy.

Annalise: And is that a no for McDonalds cookies…..? And I'm more of a basic iced caramel coffee type of person.

Me: Ewww

Annalise: Don't hate on my drink. It's delicious.

Me: If you say so.

Annalise: Shut up! I'm telling you, it's delicious. Next time I go to Starbucks I'll get you one. I wanted to tell you something btw.

Me: What's that?

Annalise: What you did today was awesome. That kid's a dick, and you were totally right, even though you were kind of wrong for hitting him. But then again if anyone deserved to get hit. . .

Me: It was him, for sure. And thanks. I didn't want to act like that, you know. Especially in front of you.

Annalise: Why not in front of me?

Me: I don't know. I just. . .I just didn't wanna give the wrong impression.

Annalise: And what impression do you think I have of you?

Me: I don't know. You'd have to tell me.

Annalise. Okay. Maybe one day I will. But seriously, how do you feel about skipping school tomorrow?

Me: I'm down if I get to hang out with you.

Annalise: One question then. . .

Me: What?

Annalise: Do you like nature?

Interlude

———————

ON BEING JUST ANOTHER MIXED UP MIXED KID.

What do I mean by mixed up mixed kid, you ask? We'll get to the mixed up part in a second, but as far as the mixed kid thing goes, well. . .let's just say that my racial and ethnic background confused the living hell out of people, especially when I was a kid. When I say confused you probably think I'm exaggerating for dramatic effect, but explaining that shit to people was like explaining how an airplane flies to someone who doesn't understand math or physics, they just looked at me and nodded, and then tried to classify me the way that was comfortable to them. I mean, I get it. I had a Spanish name, I looked vaguely tan, and I had some weird hair that was neither straight nor kinky, but some hybrid of the two. I don't know if you've ever been asked the strange question of "What are you?", but I have. *Black father, mixed mother,* I'd tell them, *but she only really identifies as Latina. Yeah, Puerto Rican, actually. No, she was born in this country. No, I don't speak it, sorry. I don't know why my hair came out like it did, I'm not a geneticist, it's just like this, I'm sorry. My hair's weird, I have no control over it.*

51

And as far as the mixed up part? By the time I was seventeen I'd just about had it with all the so-called conventional wisdom that had been imparted on me by those who'd survived long enough to have some authority over me. And the type of conventional wisdom that was forced on kids seemed particularly suspect in my experience. What do I mean? Well, let's examine the greatest lies parents tell their kids:

Be yourself. People will like you. After all, how couldn't they? There's no bias on our part, son, even though we literally created you out of thin air, and therefore think you're basically a unicorn birthed of your mom's loins who can do or say no wrong. No, everyone will love you for who you are, no matter what.

Now this may have been sound advice for those cookie cutter kids who walked, talked, and looked just like everyone else, but for someone like me? I should have been sat down and forced to write the following over and over in one of those old-school marble notebooks until it had been internalized in my little mind:

Son, while everyone should love you for who you are, most people won't. They'll find you a little odd, a little too quiet, a little too apt to tell the truth no matter what. But don't worry, life isn't a game of quantity, and for some people, like you, it's about sorting through everyone until you find the handful of people who will actually love you for who you are. That process won't be easy, son, and sometimes it'll just plain suck, but if you know that up front, maybe it'll suck a little less. Good luck, we'll try to help you whenever we can, but mostly you'll be on your own.

By the time I hit high school, I was sick of being who everyone else wanted or needed me to be. I used to think, *couldn't I just, you know, be me? Isn't that enough?* Usually it wasn't. But sometimes, I realized, you actually do find that person that your parents should have told you existed, the one who'll love you for who you are, the one who'll see the real You underneath the You that the rest of the world sees.

For that person, who you are isn't just acceptable and it isn't just good enough, who you are is everything.

THREE

Where I encounter two potential serial
killers, nearly freeze to death while sitting
on some rocks, and learn the complexities
of the word potato.

So there I was, a truant, sitting in front of Anna's place, waiting to take her to some undisclosed location as we skipped school together. We had ended our conversation the previous night around 9:00 p.m. After she texted me the most random text ever, I replied equally randomly with:

Yeah, absolutely, I love nature. Why?

To which Annalise texted back:

There's a place I know, not too many people, really beautiful. Thought maybe you could pick me up and we'd go. If you wanted to, that is.

Of course I wanted to go, which I texted back before agreeing to pick her up the following morning when we would normally be going to school. As neighborhoods went, the one Anna and I lived in was weird. Not Stephen King, small town weird - no killer clowns in the drains killing kids or vampires buying up real estate, nothing like that. But it was a place that had changed a lot in a short amount of time, and in many ways it was like two neighborhoods in one. About twenty years before I found myself parked outside of her home, the streets where Anna's house sat were completely undeveloped. My parents told me once that the whole area used to be real live farms. A local politician had made housing low income families his platform for getting elected, and the entire area on the other side of our high school had been transformed from farm land into a neighborhood of cheaply constructed, cookie-cutter row houses where poorer people lived. They'd rezoned the school district not long after the housing development was built, so there was this weird mix at our high school of kids who came from all different backgrounds and social classes.

The whole situation had caused all the problems you'd imagine happening when low income families sent their kids to the same school as upper middle class families sent theirs. Most of that tension had come and gone by the time I went to pick Annalise up, but I wondered how growing up in that neighborhood had given her a very different life than I had just a few blocks over. Everything was different in that part of town. The houses were smaller, and subdivided among different families, the stores sold cheaper items, and whenever you heard a cop or fire siren vaguely in the distance it was usually headed over there. As I sat in sociological contemplation, she walked out of her house staring at her phone, and as I watched her come towards the car I had two unrelated thoughts:

Thought 1: She was clearly the most beautiful girl who'd ever lived up to that point in history, hands down, no argument and. . .

Thought 2: I wondered how the hell she didn't trip or bump into something as she walked staring at her phone

She seemed able to navigate the street like a blind person whose other senses have been heightened, like some straight Daredevil shit. As she got closer to the car

Thought 2 faded away, and Thought 1 became more and more acute, because her face had me mesmerized, even while she was looking down, and I got lost in the sway of her hair, and in the way she shifted her weight back and forth while wearing her jet black, knee-high boots. I should've stopped staring, I was descending into creep mode fast and I didn't want to freak her out. Not that she would have noticed, she was still staring down at her phone, so I stole a few more seconds before she got in the car.

Sometimes during the really important moments in my life I experienced what I used to call slow motion moments. They were basically the times where the time in my head and actual time didn't overlap, when I could have a whole inner dialogue in my messed up mind while in actuality only ten seconds had passed back on Earth. Sounded like science fiction, right, like the lamest Marvel superhero power ever, but it happened all the time for real. One of those moments happened that morning, as I watched Annalise walk towards my car. In what must have taken about fifteen seconds of normal people time I had a slow motion moment. In it my own voice echoed in my mind, and it whispered to her,

So we're finally somewhere, together. If you were to look up at me I probably wouldn't look excited but, like they say, looks can so easily deceive. It's 6:30 in the morning after all, and this Dunkin Donuts coffee just isn't doing anything for me, but I didn't need any caffeine to get my heart and mind racing. I don't need anything at all because I'm here with you, and that's everything. I doubted we'd even make it here. How my heart fell into my stomach when I finally answered your email and texts, but here we are. You're the most beautiful girl I've ever seen in my life. I can't just blurt that out the moment I see you, but it's all I can think of as I look at you. It's all I ever think when I look at you... You're so beautiful, and you've chosen to be here with me... I didn't really wake up this morning, because this doesn't happen to me. This doesn't happen at all. I'm asleep and dreaming, and I never want to wake up.

"Hey," I said as she finally got in the car, "What's up?"

"Potato."

"Huh?"

"Potato," she repeated in a softer tone than the first time. I was totally confused and she had only been in the car for five seconds.

"You want a potato?" I asked, not yet being schooled in the ways she used that term. The look on her face didn't change one bit when I asked, but she was looking right into my eyes, as if to study my reaction. I was thrown off by her eye contact. Her eyes were this deep, magical sort of brown, and they robbed me of my ability to think properly. I continued to stammer, "I mean, I can…get you a potato, if you want a potato. There's a grocery store…"

"So let's go," she interrupted. I'm not sure what just happened, or if she actually wanted a potato, but I was fully prepared to plant and harvest potatoes if need be. It might have taken a season or so, but I would have gotten it done for her. She grinned, and I started driving, realizing that she was joking.

Pause the narrative. Hit the brakes. We don't need a full interlude here but let me tell you all about this word she used. She said potato to confuse me, but sometimes she said it because she didn't know what else to say. It could be filler, the way some people say 'umm' when they need time to process before speaking. Other times it meant that she was happy. Sometimes she said it when she was sad as hell, too. It was confusing; don't ask me any follow up questions because the truth is I don't know why she used that word. I don't know if it was something she did with everyone or just something she did with me, but to this day I can't hear the word potato without thinking of her. Like I said, complexity. Back to the story. . .

"So, where am I going?" I asked.

"Just start driving, I'll let you know."

We started driving to I didn't know where, and from time to time she gave me a verbal direction (*go left, turn right, get in the left lane, the exit's coming up*) and a few times she just did the nonverbal point to a parkway sign I was meant to pay particular attention to. We drove for about fifteen minutes or so, making some small talk along the way, with me wondering just where the hell I was going.

"That really was amazing yesterday," she said again.

"Oh, thanks. Got me in a little trouble, though. And now I'm in double trouble."

"Right, ISS."

"Yeah, our school's answer to the prison industrial complex. Have you ever been?"

"Once," she said. "It was awful."

"What'd you do?"

"I called my Earth Science teacher a bitch. It was wrong of me, but she kinda was. At least she was with me."

"How come?" I asked. "What did she do?"

"It was more about how she spoke to me. I wasn't like the other kids. She called me Emo." I laughed and Anna didn't know why. "What's funny?"

"I got that the other day, too. My homeroom teacher."

"These teachers need to come up with some new expressions. It's like anyone who isn't happy all the time is some damaged teenager who needs a label. Do they not remember what it was like in high school? Were they walking around with huge Joker grins on their faces all day?"

"They definitely don't remember," I said. "If they did they wouldn't say things like that. I bet they were pretty Emo themselves. They just have that adult amnesia where they forgot everything that they ever did or felt before they got full time jobs and families."

"Adult amnesia, I like that. Do you think that'll happen to us one day?"

"I hope not," I said. "But who knows. I'm sure they never thought it would happen to them either. I guess they just started living in that real world they keep telling us we're about to move to after high school."

"I hate that, too. My life is pretty real."

"Same."

"Why'd you react so angrily, though? You don't seem like the guy who just starts fights like that."

"Are you saying I'm a wimp?"

"If I thought that about you I wouldn't be in the car. From what I can tell you're anything but. I'm just asking because you seem gentle. You can be tough and gentle at the same time, you know."

Tough and gentle. I liked the contrast of that. "Thanks," I said. "Touchy subject. He hit a nerve with what he said and I just saw red. I don't like acting like that, however much he may have deserved the beating."

"Maybe you'll tell me more about it when we get where we're going. It's a place that almost begs you to talk."

I didn't know what she meant, but about five minutes later I pulled off exit 30 on the parkway we were driving down. "Here?" I asked. She nodded. "Where are we, exactly?"

"The rocks," she answered.

"Oh, okay, sure. Why not," I said. She smiled.

I saw a series of parking spots that overlooked the most beautiful body of water. When I pulled into one of the spots I saw the rocks. On the edge of the water sat a few hundred feet of giant stones that fit into one another like a naturally occur-ring jigsaw puzzle that looked directly onto the sparkling water. "So when you said rocks you meant rocks, huh?"

"Yeah," she said. "I love this place. It's *my* place."

Even though it was a beautiful morning, I realized right away that I should have dressed more warmly. I was wearing a long sleeved tee shirt and a thin jacket, but I could still feel the autumn air pretty intensely. As we got out of the car I felt a powerful gust of wind, and the second it hit me I felt the cold get inside of me, but Annalise didn't seem to notice, so I pretended not to also. We approached the rocks together and I couldn't help but notice how beautiful she looked in that light, how the sun hit her in just the right way to accentuate everything that was amazing about her face. *How did we get here*, I asked myself, realizing that it was both a literal and figurative question, and it occurred to me how easily this opportunity could have been missed. What if good-old Mr. A had grouped us differently for his dumb project? What if he didn't ask us to exchange contact information with each other? A thousand 'what-if's', but who cared, I was there with her, and the what-if's were irrelevant.

"It's really pretty here," I said as we stood in front of the car. It was pretty early in the day, so most people were either on their way to work or rotting their brains away in a classroom somewhere. We were doing neither. We'd stolen this moment for us, and the rest of the world wasn't invited.

"It's the best. You ready?"

"Ready for what?"

"To go out."

"Out where?

She pointed out onto the rocks themselves. "To the

rocks. That's the best part. There's plenty of room to sit, don't worry."

"Why would I be worried? Let's do it. You lead the way." I was so full of shit it was coming out of my ears. I didn't bother to mention that I was terrified of the water because I never learned how to swim, that it scared me so much that I had to look elsewhere to not have a panic attack right then and there. But I wasn't about to express any sort of fear. Instead I just followed her, watching her move fluidly from stone to stone in those crazy ass heels she wore. Girl was a gazelle on those rocks, navigating the terrain like someone who knew it well, carefully avoiding the gaps where the rocks met and countless people surely sprained their ankles. To avoid anxiety I kept my eyes fixed on the back of her feet, on the heels of those boots, and moved my feet to mirror her. We walked in lock-step, and every now and again I'd look down into those cracks to see the garbage people left there. "So, you wanna stop here?" I asked, noticing how far we'd gone down the strip.

"I'm going all the way to the end," she said without even turning around. The gust of the wind made her declaration almost inaudible. The end, as she put it, was already occupied by two random men dangling fishing poles into the water. I couldn't see them too clearly, but I knew that I didn't want to go anywhere near their shady asses, so I attempted to talk her out of it.

"There are some people down there already, why don't stop here and talk?" She stopped and turned around.

"I like people," she said. "I like talking to new people, let's keep going and talk to them, what do you think their names are?"

"Thing is, they're probably serial killers, and they come here every day waiting for teenaged girls to come hang out and ask their names, at which point they'll ask if you want to help them fish. You'll say *yes*, of course, because you're friendly, at which point they'll blindfold you, kidnap you and you'll end up bound and screaming in their basement."

"I will not," she said causally. "No, they're nice, I can tell. I think the one on the left is named John. He looks like a John, I'm gonna go ask him." Paying no attention to my elaborate sarcasm and dark humor, she started to walk towards the serial killers.

"Seriously, how about here?" I asked, stopping in my tracks and motioning down to the rock below my feet. She turned and faced me, and I could see her studying my face. I really didn't want to go to the end; people freaked me out in general, and strange fishing men on rocks even more so, particularly if there was a reasonable chance they'd chop us up into pieces.

"Okay," she conceded. "Here's good." I couldn't tell if she did that for me, or if she never really intended to befriend the strange men on the rocks to begin with. Regardless, we stopped and sat down. I became more aware of the wind, and how cold it was making me, as it blew from what seemed like every direction at once. I look at Annalise, but she stared off into the distance.

"Why would you think those guys are killers?"

"Because it's not even 8 o'clock in the morning and they're doing that. Don't need more evidence than that. It's practically the beginning of an episode of *Law & Order*. So do you come here a lot?" I asked. "How did you even find this place?"

"My sister brought me here one night with her boyfriend. After that I started coming here on my own. Usually when I'm feeling bad late at night."

"You come here at night? Are there other people here?"

"Yeah, depending on the day, it can either be like it is right now or crawling with kids. Couples, mostly."

"I can see that. It seems like a romantic spot."

"I just come to get away," she said. "It helps me clear my mind."

"Well it's good that you have a place like this. Thanks for bringing me here."

"You don't have to thank me, you know. I'm happy to be here with you." I was a little shocked by her words. I realize now that I had built her up so much in my mind to the point that she'd become mythological. Everything good that happened between us was met by some kind of disbelief on my part at first, like, how the hell could she be happy to be here with me? Sometimes insecurity just screamed in my ear because it got bored. We sat quietly for a minute, just taking in the geography and breathing in the air. I was still freezing, but I kept that to myself a little longer.

"It's my turn to ask you something."

"Okay," she said, finally making eye contact.

"What was with all that dropping out stuff? I mean, I get it, I hate school too, trust me. But we're in our last year. Why would you even consider that?"

She paused after I asked that, as though she was choosing just the right words to express herself. And then she spoke, looking me right in the eye. "I've just been having some issues at home," she said, "I kind of mentioned them in the email a little bit."

"I know the feeling," I said. "You don't have to talk about it if you don't want to."

"No. I told you, this is the place for words. You can say whatever you want here because the wind carries your words and thoughts away, and they float along to a place where they can't hurt you anymore."

"But what if they're good thoughts?"

"I'll let you know," she said. "I've never tried." Then she started telling me about things that I'm sure she wished the wind would have taken away. She was super open with me that day, even though, at that point the totality of our time together included her witnessing an assault on my part and sitting on some big rocks together. She told me that her mom had been having some psychological problems the last few years and took them out on Annalise on bad days; how her and her sister didn't really get along, and how the combined stress of all this unwarranted life experience had given her a few issues of her own that she was dealing with. I listened closely to everything she said, and its familiarity wasn't lost on me at all. At the same time I felt really happy that she chose to share that part of herself with me. We both had sick moms, and we both had responsibilities most teenagers didn't have to even think about. All of a sudden I felt very close to her, even though she knew none of the specifics of my own home drama.

"I'm sorry you're going through all that," I said.

"It's okay, I'll live."

"Yeah, I know you'll live, trust me I know all about that, but it still sucks and I'm sorry."

"Thank you." This time she looked up from the water into my eyes, and it was a look that made me feel like she understood what I meant when I said that I was sorry. I wasn't pitying her at all, I was empathizing with her.

"It's just my *Bleh*."

"Excuse me?" I was totally confused. At first I thought she was clearing her throat, or that it was some Spanish word that fake Spanish people like myself couldn't understand, so I decided to follow up. "It's your what?"

"My Bleh. My sadness."

"Why do you call it that? Did you just make that up?"

"I don't know," she said. "I've always called it that. When you say it out loud it sounds just like how you feel when it visits you."

"Is it like depression?"

"Depression is a type of *Bleh*. But depression is some name psychologists came up with to put in a book of disorders. The *Bleh* is older than that, it existed in one form or another long before there were words like depression."

"You sound like you've given this a lot of thought."

"Well, when you feel something a lot you kind of have to think about it. It's always on your mind. I just gave it a sound."

I'd never heard it expressed quite like that before, but it made total sense. "So does it visit you often?"

"There are different types," she explained. "Sometimes it's a mild *Bleh*, the kind of thing that only lasts a little while, like a mild cold. But other times it's the flu, and it kind of takes over your whole mind and doesn't let go until it feels like it. Those are the bad ones. It just depends."

It was a strange and perfect explanation. And Anna was right. Depression was just a word, but feelings existed long before there were words to describe them, and I understood exactly what she was describing. I wondered what kind of *Bleh* my mom had. It had to be a bad one.

"But enough about me. Tell me about your drama?"

"That's a long story," I said, looking away for the first time.

"I have a few minutes," she joked. "Plus I want to know. I want to know all about you."

My first impulse when she asked about my problems was to go to my script—the lines I recited at moments like that—but that impulse lasted only a second or two, because I realized that for the first time in years I actually wanted to talk to someone about it, someone who could understand where I was coming from. "Okay," I said.

I told her everything I could possibly tell while freezing my ass off on some rocks. All broad strokes: mom's breakdown, dad walking out the door, me taking on more shit than any teenager should ever have to take on, all of it. She listened closely, never looking away from me, and it was my turn to stare into the water.

"So how is she now?" Anna asked.

"You know how it is," I said back, not wanting to answer her question.

"Yeah, I know how it is," she said, touching my face and turning it towards hers. "But I want you to tell me how it is for *you*."

"It's rough," I said, feeling more than a little emotional. "I'm kind of stuck between a rock and a hard place, no pun."

"Are you calling me a hard place?" she asked, smiling.

"Absolutely not," I joked. "It's like I hate school *and* I hate being home, and I feel so guilty saying that, but it's the truth. It's sad as hell being around depression all the time. She doesn't get better, I just get worse. It's like the opposite of what should happen."

"You'll be okay," she said. "You're strong." She placed her hands on my shoulder, and I looked up at her. "I can tell that about you already."

"I know we don't know each other that well, but I think you're the strong one between the two of us."

She smiled again, and I couldn't help but notice how attentive she was to what I was saying. She was complex, and the more time we spent together, the more I thought about how her beauty was the least remarkable thing about her. She was sarcastic, intelligent, troubled, and as old of a soul as I was. And to think that for an entire year all I saw was the pretty girl. I was a fool, there was so much more to her, and I didn't know the half of it. I wanted to know everything, and I wanted to tell her everything about me.

"So what are you going to do next year after school's over?

"Shhh," she said, putting her index finger to her lips. It was a surreal moment, not only because I can't remember being shushed before, but also because I let her do it to me. Had it been almost anyone else I would have interpreted that as rude, but she wasn't anyone else, she wasn't most people, and the normal rules of who I was didn't seem to apply to her, especially in a moment where she was being vulnerable with me. "I'm sorry," I said, "I didn't mean to—"

"No, it's ok," she interrupted gently, "Sensitive topic. I don't wanna talk about that right now, I'm sorry. I didn't mean to be rude."

"We don't have to talk about anything you don't want to. Weird as it sounds I'm having a good time."

"Me too," she said back. "And it doesn't sound weird at all." Before I could say anything else she noticed that I was shivering, although I was trying my hardest to hide it. Then I understood that it was a fool's errand to try and hide anything from her; she seemed to have this eye that reached past any façade or lie I attempted to put in front of her. It was disarming and disconcerting all at once. "Wait, you're cold?" she asked in a voice that sounded genuinely concerned.

"Nah, I'm alright, it's really nice out," I lied. My lies became like verbal quicksand; the more I struggled the deeper I sank.

"No, you're cold, why didn't you tell me before?" I told her that I wasn't about to interrupt her story to complain about a little wind. And plus, I wasn't as fragile as all that.

"Come on," she said as she picked herself up from the rocks. "Let's go back to the car." I tried to protest a little, to let her know that I was fine, and that we could stay there as long as she wanted to, but she wasn't having any of it. We made our way back to my car and I blasted the heat to its highest setting the second after the key was in the ignition. "See," she said, annoyed, "you *were* cold. I can't believe you didn't tell me, I wouldn't have taken you out there!"

"I'm sorry," I said. "I didn't want to ruin the moment."

"Don't ever apologize about how you feel. Ever."

"Is that better?" she asked as I warmed my hands on the heating vents.

"Getting there. I think I'm getting some feeling back in them now."

"Maybe this will help," she said reaching over and putting her hands over mine, and I felt electricity that burned hotter than the heat in the car could have ever created. She rubbed both of my folded hands with hers in the most loving of ways, and her palms brought the sensation back to my fingertips. As she held onto me I thought of how the two of us were seen by so many people every day, yet still not really seen at all for who we really were. We didn't wear our stories on our sleeves, we just looked like your everyday, average teenagers. And we were. But as cliché as it sounded, we were like icebergs; most of who we were was far beneath the surface.

I hadn't seen Annalise for who she was all of those months I loved her from afar. I was just being superficial, seeing all the dumb things teenaged boys see—her face, her smile, her body—but I hadn't seen her. She was just like me and nothing like me, all at the same time. It was like we were invisible, sort of. No one saw her just like nobody really saw me, like the world around us was blind.

"Potato," I said to her as the frostbite feeling left my hands.

"No."

"Wait, what? Did I use it wrong?" I asked.

"Only I can say that," she informed me, in no uncertain terms. "You don't know how to use it yet."

"Oh, okay. I didn't know that there were rules?"

"There are always rules, Logan, even if you don't know what they are, and you just broke one of them. Only I can say potato. You don't use it right at all. I mean, you can say it, but only if you're like, talking about an actual potato."

"So, what are the other rules?" I asked. "Do I need a booklet to explain them all to me?"

"I can't tell you the rules, silly. You just have to pick up on them as we go."

"I see. No potato, got it. Should I write these down?" She smiled at me and giggled. "So, you're not gonna drop out, right?" I asked.

"Yeah, about that, why were you so nice to me about that whole thing?"

"Well, I told you, my mom—"

"Right," she interrupted, "But why?" I looked at her confused.

"What do you mean?"

"Like, why me?" At that point she was making intense eye contact; the opposite of how she'd been while we sat on the rocks, and it's like her stare was holding me, and I couldn't look away. It was distrustful eye contact, as if she were evaluating if I had ulterior motives. "Like, you barely know me," she continued. "So why?" She had a point, at least from her point of view. In the absence of her knowing about my not-so-minor, yearlong obsession, it probably seemed a little weird that I was being so nice. Plus, I was a guy, and even at our age girls learned that most guys had ulterior motives to their kindness.

"I don't know, because I care." It was all I could think to say, I hadn't expected her to question me like that, and the pressure made me nervous.

"Right, okay, but why? Why do you care? There are a lot of kids with problems at school. Do you care about all of them?"

"Not really, no."

"So why, then? Why me? What's so special about me?" Normally if a beautiful girl had asked me something like that I would have assumed that she was looking for a laundry list of compliments to come out of my mouth. Annalise was different, like really different, she seemed to genuinely not understand why I would care about her.

"I don't know…I care about you. I've….I've always cared about you." I have to look away when I say that part. Of all the scenarios I might have envisioned for a moment like that, basically confessing that I liked her wasn't one of them. But there I was, baring my soul with little more than a prompt from her; this girl was like human truth serum; I felt like I had to answer whatever question she had with complete, unfiltered honesty. I began to look up to see her reaction. Maybe she was freaked out, or maybe I needed to say more to cover my tracks. "What I meant is—" Before I finished my sentence her lips were on mine. I was in such disbelief that I held my mouth in place, like a little baby learning how to kiss. *Annalise was kissing me!* She pulled back as quickly as she had leaned in, and made that intense eye contact again, and I was transfixed on her gaze.

"Don't worry, I'm not dropping out," she said. Before I could respond she curled up into a ball and said, "I'm so tired, I barely slept last night." I couldn't think of anything appropriate to say, so I just went with the flow of this odd conversation.

"Oh, I'm sorry, what time did you go to sleep last night?" Small talk. Perfectly normal after the girl you've loved for a year took you to some secret rock water place and kissed you in your car.

"I don't know, like 4:00 am or so, I lost track."

"4! That was like a few hours ago, no wonder you're tired. What were you doing all night?"

"It's irrelevant," she said. I didn't even know what that meant, but I went with it because my head was still spinning from that kiss.

"Oh, okay, never mind. I guess I'd be tired, too."

Without lifting her head, she whispered, "You know, I care about you too. I wouldn't have ever brought you here if I didn't."

"I didn't even know that you knew who I was."

"Well I do. I have for a while now."

"Wait, how?"

"Class," she said. "School in general, but class specifically. I notice things about people, whether I seem like I'm in my own world or not, and I noticed how sad you looked in class one day."

I thought about it for a moment and I couldn't remember when or what she was talking about. "I don't remember," I told her.

"You wouldn't have," she said back. "I mean, you didn't look like you were about to hang yourself or anything, you just looked sad. I notice sadness. Maybe no one else sees it because they don't understand what they're looking at. I bet people asked if you were tired that day, and you probably told them that you were 'cause you didn't want to talk about it, but inside you were sad as hell.

After that I just kind of kept tabs on you here and there when I saw you around."

At that point you could've considered my mind blown. I couldn't believe that she'd been the one to notice me and not just the other way around. I started giggling.

"What's funny?" she asked me again.

"Life, sometimes," I said. "I used to do the same thing with you. I saw you all the time, but I was afraid."

"Of what?"

"Who even knows? Rejection. Fear of the unknown. Maybe you were really a beautiful fire-breathing dragon who I thought was about to say hello back to me, but really there would just be fire that expelled from your mouth and consumed me whole. You never know."

"You think I'm beautiful?"

Two reactions to that one: first, I forgot I even said that because I was in mid fantasy rant about a fire breathing dragon, and second, it was the most genuine question she'd asked me yet. She really didn't see it.

"Anna, have you seen what you look like? You're, like. . .you're the prettiest girl ever, I think."

She smiled and kissed me one more time, only this time I was ready, and I kissed her back. The feeling I had at that moment can't be described here, my humblest of apologies as your narrator, but there are some things that there are no words for, and my first real kiss with Annalise was one. Afterwards she told me that she had something to do that afternoon, and that we should probably get headed back to her house. It took less than a half hour to get home, and I pulled up in front of her place where I'd picked her up not that long ago.

"Thank you for bringing me there," I said. "Maybe now it won't just be a place for when you're feeling bad.

Maybe it'll be like our place. Our place on the rocks." She smiled back and opened the car door.

"I'd like that," she said, as she leaned into my open window. "Text me later, okay?"

"There's a question you never have to ask."

I said goodbye, and she walked away exactly as she had approached my car when I arrived; shifting weight on long black boots, staring back at the screen of her phone. That strange and wonderful morning ended much like it began: with me watching her walk, admiring her beauty, and thinking that I wanted to remember that dream forever.

FOUR

Where I tell you some sad stuff about the night It happened.

Get the tissue box ready. I'm sorry, I'm really not trying to bum anyone out, and trust me I'd love to spend another thousand pages writing all about how madly in love I was with Annalise, and I promise that Our Story will continue shortly, but you need to understand a little bit about my home life at the time I met Anna. I'll tell a joke or something at the end to lighten the mood a bit.

Do you remember that lesson in Bio about evolution? I know, we've established how stupid and forgettable high school was, but a few things do stick. I even remember my teacher's name - Mr. Johnson. Standard issue name for an extraordinary guy. Type of teacher who was an outlier by caring as much as he did. I can see his PowerPoint presentation now, a big picture taken straight from Google images of our boy Darwin, staring at the class with that serious mug he always seemed to have in every picture (seriously, Google the man, he never looks happy). I remember how Mr. Johnson gave us a reading from *On the Origin of Species* and how he taught us that the nature of evolutionary change is a gradual, almost imperceptible thing, at least while it's happening. It's kinda like how your relatives from out of town always comment on how big your kids have gotten since the last time they saw them. When you only see change once in a while it seems sudden, but that's only because we can't perceive those moments as they're happening.

Change may be gradual for species, and that all works just fine in a science textbook, but sometimes the evolution of an individual doesn't go down that way. Sometimes change is quick, violent, and as obvious as a thing can be. I couldn't tell you a damn thing about what I was doing the night that everything changed before it actually changed. I don't remember what I had for lunch, or what show I was watching on TV when I first heard the screaming from upstairs, but I remember everything that followed like that shit happened yesterday. Here's how it went down.

Memory's a strange and unknowable mystery some-times isn't it? Can't really explain why some things were lost to history and some I'd never forget if I lived to be one hundred and five years old. So the television schedule and other minutiae of that night are gone, ain't ever coming back, but the hushed fight sounds I could recall with vivid clarity. I was used to that sound, heard it my whole life, and formulated entire memories around those days and their resolutions.

I remember the time dad was changing in front of that big armoire he had in his room, and I asked him where he got those scars across his neck? Yeah, I remember that; Mom got so mad she couldn't control that Latina temper any longer and did her best impersonation of an angry tiger on good-old dad's chest. I remember all the 'talks' they used to tell me they were having, and even as a kid I knew that was bullshit 'cause their talking sounded a hell of a lot like fighting, bad fighting, angry fighting. I also knew what to do, I had lots of practice, years of it actually. Never go up to your room, that was rule number 1. Obvious one there, your room was upstairs right across from theirs, no sense in getting closer to the battle grounds, that didn't make any sense.

The only other room up there was the bathroom, and no one needed to pee that bad. That left downstairs, didn't it? Nowhere else to run and hide, so I learned what to do. Turn up the volume on the TV, but the trick was to make it loud enough to drown out the yelling, but not so loud for it to be obvious what you were doing. If you interrupted their 'talk' with some forced parental discipline about the television being too damn loud, you just knew they were going to overreact. No, had to do it just right, loud enough to make the sound of their marital fury a muffled buzz on the periphery of your consciousness. That was enough; enough to bear the slow, decades long harmonies of a marriage committing suicide in the background. I mean, if I'm being honest I'd seen and heard worse fights, but there was always a next day; always some actual talking to accompany all the fake talking, then the cycle repeated itself at some point, like the phases of the moon. But that day was the last; that night was the closing scene of a tragedy, and it all started like any other.

Laundry.

Mom went upstairs to fold laundry. Took the basket up and everything, I can still see it rested against her hip as she took it up the stairs. Dad was up there already doing some dad shit - shaving, picking his shirt and tie for the next day, who knows. Doesn't matter. But their paths crossed in a series of unrelated tasks that led to a meeting of consequential words that break wedding vows; the kind that brought to a head decades of toxic and unhealthy patterns; the type of words that broke people.

What you really remember is how quick it was, how short. Not a bang so much as a whimper, a fight that the bigger, stronger fights would have made fun of and shoved in a locker at school. How quickly the world could change forever. Dad walked out. Mom stayed on the bed, sobbing and shaking. I'd seen sadness and dysfunction of all varieties and magnitudes, but I understood, even at fifteen, that I was seeing a different type of thing. I used to wonder if there were other sad kids like me who spent all of their energy worrying if their moms would commit suicide. I used to have these thoughts while lying awake late at night, wondering if Mom was alive in the next room; those times when the muted sobbing she tried in vain to hide from me finally quieted, I'd wonder if she snuck up a bottle of her pills and an extra-large glass of water. The sobbing disturbed, but the silence frightened, like with babies—it might be annoying when they scream, but when they're too quiet your first impulse is usually fear. My mind did its own crazy dance in that silence, and I'd envision the possible scenarios playing out in the sad bedroom. After that night everything changed. Mom became a patient, and I became her caregiver, a reversal of the natural order of life, only I still had a life of my own to attend to.

Anyway, back to Our Story. . .

I'd gotten home from being with Anna and Mom was half catatonic, a side effect of all the meds, staring out the window in her favorite chair in the living room. That was her spot. My spot, accordingly, was up in my room by my lonesome, but I didn't really like it up there. I wasn't a room kid. Most kids were room kids. What do I mean? Like that cliché, *I'm going to go be all dark and sad in my room while texting my friends and blasting music.* Wasn't me. For me it was a displacement behind enemy lines, the only safe spot within a larger territory I didn't really like spending time in, but I didn't really like it in there. In fact, as soon as I found myself staring at my four walls I was actively engaged in trying to get the hell out of there. And that meant involving Pete.

Forgetting that I was playing the role of dirt bag truant for the day, I suddenly realized that Pete was still at school, and I was the one sitting at home in the middle of the afternoon, so I decided to text. He'd write me back, even if he was in class. It was best friend code. To not do so would've been an immediate and irrevocable breach of the best friend contract we signed when we were five.

"Hey," he texted back immediately. "Where are you?"

"I've got a lot to tell you, man. What do you have right now?"

"See what happens when you get a taste of the outside world? You forget the bell schedule like you never even knew it."

"You've just been institutionalized. Don't blame me for resisting that mind control. Now what class do you have now?"

"Right now I'm sitting in math."

"So you're probably happy to be hearing from me, then. How's Mr. Krueger's sweat today?"

"Intense," he wrote back with a laughing emoji. "He's trying his hardest not to have to raise his arms, but he wants desperately to point to the equation up on the board for Jenny."

"Shit, has Jenny ever not needed fifteen recitations of the same point during a math lesson? I swear that girl needed to be classified years ago, but her family's just too embarrassed."

"These texts are getting too long," he wrote back, another laughing emoji following his text. Pete's emoji game was strong, but he overused them. I used to tell him I

79

was worried that one day he'd go full caveman and cease expressing himself with human words. He told me I was being my usual overthinking self and then we stopped talking about it. That's how our relationship was.

"I agree," I wrote. "Whatever you have the next two periods, skip it. Let's get caffeinated and talk. Like I said, a lot to tell you."

"I'm in. Side ramp of the school in fifteen?"

"Shit, I'd better get going then."

"Where are you?"

"Home," I replied. "I'm home now."

"And here I am sitting through this bullshit and you're chillin' in your room. Get dressed and get in your car, I don't wanna linger outside school for too long. You know how security guards are here."

"Think they're cops."

"Exactly," Pete wrote. "Fifteen. Don't be late."

I changed into something a little warmer, my body still chilled from the aggressive wind on the rocks. When I was done I caught myself in the mirror and I stopped for a second to stare. No, I wasn't some Narcissus-type character who liked to steal glimpses of himself whenever possible. What I realized, though, was that the Me in the mirror was different than the Me in the mirror last time I looked. That Logan was a boy, a lost soul, the loser of losers who asked the universe for things he wanted. And, to be honest, I was still most of those things, only the Now Logan had kissed Annalise, and no matter my other cosmic shortcomings, that made me proud to look at myself for a minute or two. But once I realized it was getting weird and going on for too long I broke from my dissociative madness and headed downstairs. I was hoping Mom would ignore me, but no such luck.

"Where are you headed, baby?"

"Going to meet Pete. We're getting coffee. You want me to bring you back anything?"

"You're so sweet, but no, I made some already this morning. I don't need any more caffeine."

"I can't relate," I joked, looking at her and smiling. She smiled back. She always smiled back, but it was a rehearsed sort of thing, a strained push of her cheek muscles upwards for my benefit. She looked like that scrawny dude at the gym who tried to lift too much weight to impress the other people, but deep down I appreciated the show for my benefit. She knew I'd seen too many tears. "I'll be back in a little while and we'll get something for dinner, okay?"

"Okay, baby, have a good time. Be careful driving and say hi to Pete for me. I feel like I haven't seen him in forever."

That's because you haven't. That's because no one's been here in forever. "I will. Bye." There was always a weird guilt that came with every close of my front door. I don't know, maybe I had survivor's guilt, or maybe being the only person in this world my mom had to rely on was a burden I wasn't ready to bear. Either way, I had bigger things on my mind that day, so I took my usual guilt-ridden walk away from our house, my worries about Mom overridden by my excitement to tell Pete what had happened.

I got to the school with a minute to spare from when I told Pete I'd meet him. My boy came strolling out of the side door like a seasoned school criminal, evading the overzealous security guards who goose stepped through the inside and outside of the building, eventually slipping around the passenger side of my car and hopping in next to me. "Tight move," I said as he put his seatbelt on and we watched the kids shuffle along to their next class.

"The transition," he said back, grinning like he just

captured the Hope Diamond. "It's all in the transition between classes. You've got to make your move in the chaos." He was right. Those three minutes were the absolute best time to cut out of the building, when the hallways became a human ant farm and all the kids sounded their battle cries as they made their way to wherever they were scheduled to be. Why were we so loud? Maybe it was our collective battle cry, our vocal resistance within the confines of that building. Or maybe I just thought weird shit like that while I waited for my best friend to buckle his damn seatbelt so we could get coffee.

"So," Pete began as we pulled out of the parking lot all incognito. "You're in a world of shit, huh?"

"What do you mean?"

"Well not only did you skip school but you skipped out on your jail sentence, too. Now it's gonna be doubled."

"They could quadruple it for all I care. Put my ass on high school death row. Screw it."

"Wow," Pete joked. "Someone grew a set. I like it. What's the inspiration for sticking it to the Man?"

"My only inspiration. The only one I've ever had." Pete looked over at me, methodical as all hell, like his neck was in some dramatic slow motion shot in a movie, and I knew right away that he got my meaning.

"No," he said.

"Uh-huh."

"Fuck you."

"That isn't very nice. Keep that up and I'm not paying for your coffee."

"Oh, shit, you must be telling the truth. You'd never offer to buy me coffee unless you were in a state of pure bliss."

He was right. That wasn't like me at all, but my head was still in the clouds, or on the rocks as it were, and I was happy to empty my wallet if it meant I got to gloat for once. I drove him to our favorite diner that was only a few blocks away, and even though I was somewhat of a coffee snob, even then, this place knew how to push water through a bean like no other place around. So it was only fitting that it was there, at the booth in the back where we always sat, that I told him how I'd spent my morning as he listened to lectures on World War II. He responded in typical, elegant Pete fashion.

"Bullshit."

"I shit you not, my oldest of friends. For real."

"No."

"Yes. When have I ever just bold faced lied to you."

"Never"

"That's right. So why would I start about something like this, of all things?"

Pete pondered my question. He knew I wasn't lying, and I knew that he knew I wasn't lying, but his brain needed a moment to accept the truth. If I could have been inside his head I would have seen new wrinkles forming.

"We have a lot to talk about."

"I know, why do you think I brought you here?"

"Wait, are you really paying?"

"I'm really paying."

"Sweet. Now tell me."

And that's exactly what I did, sort of. I gave him the broad strokes that best friends just needed to know, but I modified the truth to keep the parts that weren't anyone else's business to myself. I told him about the email, but I didn't mention her maybe dropping out. I told him about the rocks but not about the kiss. I told him that we talked for a long time, but I didn't get into what we actually talked about. He didn't pry, he wasn't like that.

"Here," he said, getting out of his side of the booth

and standing about as upright as I've ever seen a person do. He extended his hand to me and had this dumb grin on his face that I'll never forget.

"What the hell are you doing?" I asked, staring at him like he was as crazy as he was acting.

"Stand up, my friend, we're about to have a moment here."

"I think we're having it, people are staring, man, sit down."

"Let them stare," he said, his voice raising like he was giving a commencement speech. "Let them remember where they were on this fine day for years to come. Rise!"

I stood up just to stop him from yelling. Once I was up I couldn't stop seeing all the eyes of the random elderly people who came to diners during the day to avoid loud teenagers like us. I reached out and shook his hand and went to sit again, but he wouldn't let go. "We're not done?"

"Oh no, not even close. Everyone, an announcement," he was yelling now, and I saw the owners getting ready to come over and ask us to leave, but they weren't as quick as his tongue, which was embarrassing me with every passing syllable. "Ladies and gentlemen, your attention for a brief moment." I wanted to die. I wanted to literally crawl inside myself and disappear. "My best friend of over a decade has finally stopped being such a—"

"Stop," I yelled. "Don't finish that sentence."

"He's finally been brave enough to talk to the girl of his dreams, and that, ladies and gentlemen, deserves a round of applause." Pete started clapping uncontrollably. Loud as hell. Embarrassing. Being applauded is just like getting Happy Birthday sung to you. . .there isn't much you can do but sit there like an idiot until the thing runs its mortifying course. No one else clapped, and I wanted to run out of there screaming, but our coffee was on the way so I just grabbed Pete by the arm and pulled him down.

"Any more clapping and you're buying your own coffee."

"What, I can't be happy for my best friend? I'd say this was a big deal."

"Be happy for me quietly."

Pete joined me back in the land of the sane, deciding that making a public spectacle of us was less important than getting some free caffeine. When we were done talking he got this look on his face like one of these cartoon characters who's having a revelation. I wouldn't have been shocked if a lightbulb appeared briefly over his head. "What?" I asked.

"I have an idea."

"That's obvious. What's your idea?"

"Our month-a-versary. You guys should come with!"

This requires some explanation. Time for another brief interlude, the Pete and Lindsey edition. So remember when I said that Pete was the ladies' man of our dynamic duo? That he had all the initiative I lacked when it came to just walking up to beauty and introducing his goofy self? Well that's exactly how he met Lindsey, his high school wife. Lindsey was hot. Now I never would have said it that emphatically to Pete because he leaned towards jealous and overprotective at times, but it was the truth. Lindsey was that girl that dudes broke their neck to watch walk away, but she was down to earth and a real sweet heart. At the time of Our Story they'd been together going on eleven months, which was like a silver anniversary in adolescent relationship time. No drama, no cheating, no bullshit, just two of my favorite people in love with one another.

He'd christened their 11 month anniversary as their

11th month-a-versary, a term to this day I've only ever heard Pete use. He'd hijacked our plans to go to Comic Com together and instead tried to turn two geeks geeking out into his stupid anniversary day, dinner and hotel stay included. This last part seemed shady at best, but he'd been saving up some money to get a nice room for them to spend the night together.

"Wait," I broke in. "So you want me to go with you?"

"Not you, moron. You and Annalise."

"Like a double date?"

"No, like *the* double date. No indefinite articles here. That shit will be epic. You guys can get a room too."

"Woah, woah, slow your roll. I've literally spent one morning with the girl and now you have me taking her to dinner and a hotel. I'm honored for the invite, but I don't think that's gonna work out." Pete was impulsive like that. It didn't even occur to him that asking a girl you've spent two hours with to spend the night in a hotel room with you wasn't something you could actually do. But I'd be lying if I said I wasn't intrigued by the idea.

"Well, if you change your mind, the invitation's there."

"Much appreciated."

When we were finished I drove Pete home. I was exhausted even though it was barely the middle of the day. I got home and went back up to my room. Mom was asleep. She slept in the day a lot, both as a side effect of her medication and from a general boredom with life. It was fine with me that afternoon, because I wanted to just be alone with my thoughts. Random texts are a theme here, and just as I was settled in front of my TV I got one from none other than Annalise.

Annalise: Hey. I need to talk to you about something.
Me: What's up?
Annalise: Did I tell you about Peru?

Me: Like that it exists? I was already aware, but no you didn't mention it.

Annalise: No, not that it exists. I'm Peruvian. I don't know if you knew that. I mean, I know you know I'm Spanish, but specifically I'm Peruvian.

Me: Oh, okay.

Annalise: Anyway, my whole family is there. I'm going away for two weeks over the holiday to visit. Sorry I forgot to tell you.

Me: Oh.

Annalise: My family over there is kind of rich. Peruvian rich, anyhow. They have this big house in Lima, so it's nice to spend time there.

Me (being fake as hell): Yeah, that sounds amazing.

I hated myself right then. I was so full of false sincerity that I could smell the bullshit radiating off my phone. I wasn't happy at all. I didn't think it was amazing for her to go to Peru, so why the hell was I saying it? Habit. Politeness. Didn't wanna start a petty fight with the girl of my dreams just 'cause I was incapable of having a normal, emotional reaction to anything. But there I was, nonetheless, pretending to be a good. . .whatever I was to her. Boyfriend seemed extreme, but we sure as hell weren't just friends after what had happened. We were some undefined hybrid creature, the boundaries and limitation of which were unknown to me. That's the thing about titles. People hate on them, but they establish rules we can all follow. Like, your girlfriend or boyfriend can ask you things that your friends just can't. They can push boundaries. They can demand that you stay in the damn country while waiting for your zygote of a relationship to at least become an embryo. But us? I didn't know what I could and couldn't say, so I went with a default politeness that I knew wouldn't cause any problems.

We went back and forth a few more times, with her telling me about how excited she was to leave, and me thinking how sad I was to see her go, even for a short time. It didn't seem fair. As the conversation wound down I felt like complete dog shit, but luckily it was texting, so she couldn't really tell. Just as I'm about to say goodbye Annalise texted.

Annalise: What's the matter?

Me: Nothing, it's fine. I'm fine.

Annalise: Yeah, so what's really wrong? Because when people say that something is 'fine' it's never really fine, that's just code for something being terribly wrong but not wanting to talk about it. So what's wrong?

It frightened me a little that she seemed to know me without actually knowing me. It seemed to be like some strange magic that women have, but only certain women; only the great ones.

Me: Nothing.

Annalise: If you keep lying to me this conversation is over. Like, bye. What is it?

I felt like she should have known why I was upset. Wasn't it obvious? Wasn't it plain as day that I had such intense feelings for her, and that her jumping the country for a few weeks might hurt me?

Me: Bummed about Peru, is all. I mean, I'm happy you get to go see your family, but after today I was hoping we could spend some more time together.

Annalise: What happened today?

My heart sank. Was she crazy, or did this morning just mean nothing to her? Maybe she went to those rocks every day; maybe she brought everyone she knew there.

Annalise: I'm kidding!

My heart started beating normally again. I wasn't used

to being the one on the receiving end of the sarcasm and I didn't like it very much.

Me: Please don't scare me like that.

Annalise: I'm sorry, it was just too easy (smile emoji). I loved this morning. I loved being there with you, and I think that you're amazing. And thanks for listening to me vent, you didn't have to.

I smiled as a looked down at my phone. If only she knew how I dreamed of a morning like that, how she never, ever needed to thank me for anything, because it was me who should have been thanking her for even existing, and for allowing me to be there in that car with her. I was about to text back 'you don't have to thank me' when I stopped myself and hit the delete button until my screen was clear. Instead I thought of something I wanted to do instead; an impulse that hit me.

Me: This may sound totally random and weird, but if I wrote something for you, would you read it?

Annalise: You going to write me a book?

Me: Not a book. Not yet, anyway, I don't have enough material for a book. But something else.

Annalise: Of course, I'd love to. I bet you're a good writer. No one's ever written anything for me before.

Me: Don't get your hopes up, I don't know if it'll be any good. But it'll be from the heart, I promise.

Annalise: I'll love it.

My heart started to pound. Once upon a time, in a reality that was getting farther and farther away, I used to write stories that no one would ever read. I put everything down on paper. Every dumb sci-fi short story, every *Lord of the Rings* knockoff (yes I did create a more complex and sophisticated language than Elvish, and no you'll never get to read it), everything I had in my crazy adolescent head would eventually find its way onto a piece of paper or my phone for an audience of zero, but it had been a long time since I'd done anything worth mentioning. And even though I hadn't had the impulse to write anything outside of the bullshit school papers and essays I was assigned, that night I was inspired; I was inspired by Annalise. I hated that word normally. It seemed like everyone was constantly talking about how inspired they were to do this or that; the word was overused. But I couldn't think of a better word, because what I felt inside was inspiration.

Me: Ok, great, well, goodnight then. I'll email it to you when I'm done, okay?

Annalise: Okay. You know we don't have to email each other anymore.

Me: This might be too long for a text.

Annalise: Got it. Night.

Game on. I was nervous that I'd built it up too much. Called my shot, Babe Ruth style. My thumbs hung just above the keyboard of my Notes app, waiting to strike the right keys. I stayed in that posture for about thirty seconds, waiting for the feelings to transform into words and for the words to transform into sentences. Funny how it all came flooding back to me, as I sat with fingers poised. The words came.

I realized right away after we pulled up that I was underdressed. I also realized how easily I would give up control to you, because I trusted you. I didn't know that after a few minutes of driving I'd be pretending to not shake uncontrollably as I squatted on a bunch of cold rocks overlooking that beautiful water. I also didn't know that I'd be inadvertently saving your life by keeping you from talking to those obvious serial killers pretending to be fishermen. So I guess in that way we're even. I rescued you from a newspaper headline that would have eventually been made into a gripping episode of Law & Order, and you saved me from the prison of school. The truth is that it wouldn't have mattered if I knew about the cold, though. I would have sat naked on frozen tundra if you asked me to. I would have gone anywhere and done anything that you asked me to.

Isn't it funny how easily we could have missed each other; how our morning on the rocks could have easily never happened. It's funny how it seems almost meant to be, even though I don't believe in that sort of thing. I know people find that romantic and all, but I look at it differently. I look at a lot of things differently. If there really were fate, and we really were meant to be there, then the story's already written, and some magical force preordained everything to happen. I find more comfort in randomness. Think about it. Of all the possibilities, of all the 'what if' scenarios, or all the variables that could have kept us apart, you still found me and I still found you. That's so much cooler than fate. Randomness gives a big middle finger to the odds sometimes.

There's this specific way that you looked when you turned away from me, an expression that framed your entire face and made me wonder just what you were thinking and feeling at that moment. I wondered what you were thinking when your eyebrow shot up just a little bit, framing your deep brown eyes as your cheeks bent upwards to meet them. I had seen smiles on other people's faces a thousand times, but yours was different. Your smile matters to me. I want to find out what I said or did to have you make that face, and then I want to repeat it forever. I've never written an actual love letter that I've given to a girl—don't think I'm very good at it. I'm sorry because you deserve better, but it's all I have to give you now, and I hope it means something special to you.

Our time on the rocks was only the beginning.

I hit the send button, and after I did I realized that there were tears in my eyes. I hadn't meant to cry; hadn't even known it was happening until I felt the downward momentum rushing down my cheek. I hadn't been able to cry in a very long time; not that I wanted to. The last thing my household needed was another person with overactive tear ducts, so I learned to hold it in. Mom got to cry. I just bought the tissues. But I couldn't stop it from happening after I had written to Annalise. I felt happy to have been crying. I wasn't sad, I felt. . .alive.

After my brief elation, I felt a more familiar feeling—panic. I had just sent Annalise, the girl I'd wanted obsessively for 365 days of my life; the girl who I stood like a moron in my tub praying to the empty sky for; the girl who filled my soul with a reason for being…I just sent her a long-ass love letter that I typed on my phone. I felt light-headed. I closed my eyes because it was the only thing I could think of doing at the time, and I laid on my bed feeling only the rapidity of my heart in my chest. I couldn't perceive just how long I laid there attempting to bring my heart rate down to a normal pace. When I panicked, which was often, time lost all sense of meaning. It was like in a dream, where you wake up feeling like you were dreaming all night, only to learn that it was most likely 10 minutes. My luck being what it was, at the exact moment I began to calm, the vibration of my phone snapped me back into anxious reality. In my heightened state, the text message double vibration seemed to shake the entire room.

When I opened my eyes to look at the clock I saw that 30 minutes had passed since I laid down. 30 minutes. As I heard the double vibration repeat itself, I realized that 30 minutes was what Annalise needed to realize that I was a needy creep; 30 minutes was all it took for her to read over my sappy bullshit, get scared, realize that I'm an asshole and that she was wasting her time with me, and to figure out a way to let me down easy. The text probably started with "…well, it was really sweet, but…" Screw it. I reached for my phone and entered my password. As the screen unlocked I refused to look down, instead choosing to stare at the cracking white paint of my ceiling. I wiped what remained of the clammy, anxiety sweat from my brow, feeling a new layer forming, and I wondered about the exact moment I had turned my dream into a waking nightmare. When I finally mustered the courage to look down, her text read:

Annalise: It took me 20 minutes to read it and re-read it over and over again…you're amazing for writing that for/about me. You don't compare to anyone else. I wish I could express my emotions but it's hard…but I will tell you how happy and smiley and just…I don't know…but it's a great feeling. I couldn't stop smiling reading the email.I knew I made a good choice by taking you there.

Me: I'm…I'm really glad that you liked what I wrote.

As I began to write my heart steadied, and I felt like I felt as I was writing to her; calm, self-assured, loved, and only slightly scared. And I also felt something else that was hard to put my finger on. It was a sort of strange and unnatural comfort that came when I spoke to her. I should have been terrified, I should have been afraid that her next words would have destroyed me, but I wasn't, I was just happy to tell her exactly what I felt inside.

Me: I thought it might have sucked. Glad it didn't. I got kind of emotional a few times as I was writing it.

Annalise: Did you really?

Me: Yeah, that's why it took so long to write.

Annalise: Not gonna lie I teared up a little while I read it.

Me: Oh, wow, so I guess we both cried a little.

Annalise: Potato

This time I was less baffled, I was starting to understand the meaning. Smiling ear-to-ear, I wrote back.

Me: Potato

Annalise: No, that's my word, remember?

Me: Right, forgot, I'm sorry. Won't happen again, promise.

Annalise: Don't promise.

Me: But I promise I won't say potato.

Annalise: Don't promise. What if you can't follow through? There's nothing worse in the whole world than a broken promise.

Me: I'm pretty sure I can restrain myself from saying potato, unless I'm talking about actual potatoes, and why would I talk to you about real potatoes?

Annalise: Well who knows where all this will take us? We could very well end up in a situation in which talking about real potatoes is necessary. You just never know, so don't promise.

Me: Okay, I don't promise.

Annalise: Oh, so now you're saying you'd lie to me?

Me: Wait, what?

She texted a smile emoji back to me.

Me: So...what happens now?

Annalise: Tomorrow? Cut school again?

Me: Of course, tomorrow it is. 7:15?

Annalise: Perfect.

After agreeing on the time we stopped talking for the night. It was time to go to sleep. I closed my eyes and allowed that day to be archived in my personal history, and no matter how hard I tried, I couldn't peel the smile from my face. Then came the well-deserved sleep, and the promise of Annalise the next day.

FIVE

Where I watch a film of us in my head.

The next morning we went back to our place on the rocks. I picked Anna up at her house like last time, and again she traversed the bumpy street from her front door to my car without an upwards glance, like a ninja, staring at her phone until she was sitting next to me.

"I'm exhausted," she said when she got in. "I didn't sleep at all."

"Me either. But then again I don't think I've slept well in a few years."

"Bad dreams?" she asked.

"Something like that," I answered, looking away. "Sometimes it's bad dreams, but mostly I just can't get to sleep at all until really late."

"I know what you mean," she told me. "I stay up till 4 or 5 a lot."

"You win," I joked. "I think my record is one or two in the morning at worst."

"Well, aren't we two peas in an insomnia pod."

"I guess we are. What's your reason for not sleeping?"

"Besides the craziness in my house?" she asked,

sounding a little sarcastic. "I share a room with my older sister, and she comes and goes all hours of the night. Plus I can't sleep if there's any light in the room and when she gets home from work or being out with her boyfriend the first thing she does is turn her lamp on. Then there are other times my mom is ranting or raving about whatever. It's a miracle I sleep at all."

"That sounds like a rough situation," I told her. I didn't really know what to say. This wasn't unique to my interactions with Anna, either. I basically never knew what to say when people complained about things in their life. Saying *oh that sucks* seemed rehearsed and soulless, but I never knew what else to say.

"I'll live. What about you?"

"Let's get on the road and I'll tell you." While we continued to bond over our mutual sleeping issues I pulled out and started driving towards the parkway. I still needed her to guide the way or we would have likely ended up stranded in New Jersey, God forbid. It was another cold day, but this time I'd come prepared with a jacket.

"So what's your blood type?" she asked out of the silence we had been sitting in a moment sooner. I'd come to love her random questions, and she asked them a lot. I realized later that they weren't random at all, they were her way of getting to know me, but her sense of context was about as strong as my sense of direction, so the questions came out of left field most times.

"Umm… I actually don't know, to be honest. How come?"

"Just curious." That was the expression she used whenever I asked why she wanted to know whatever random piece of information she wanted to know. In the last day, either in person or over text she'd asked me the following random questions like I was on a gameshow:

1. My blood type
2. My favorite animal
3. My favorite color
4. My favorite food

They all involved my favorite something or other. I'm sure that she was curious about my preferences in colors or foods, or whatever, but I wondered what thought ran through her head while we were talking about school, or family, or any other topic and she asked me something like that. At what point did complaining about a teacher, or gossiping about other kids in the school lead her down a mental path of wondering my blood type? I decided that this time I'd push a little further because I wanted to know.

"What made you think of that?" I asked her playfully. "My blood type, I mean."

"Just curious."

"Yeah, but like, were you thinking about something involving blood?" The question sounded as ridiculous out loud as it did in my head, but I didn't know how else to ask a follow up question. She gave me a funny look and grinned

"So you think that I think about blood a lot?"

"No," I said. "That's not what I meant, I'm sure you don't think. . ." Before I was finished she jumped in in that same tone of voice.

"So you're saying I think about blood, like I'm weird and dark? Okay, I see, it's fine."

I took a minute to look at her, even as I had no idea how close I was to the exit for the rocks. She's squared her body off to mine, putting her back against the window and making intense eye contact with me even though I wasn't looking back most of the time. Even though I only saw it for a second before looking back at the road, the look on her face made me feel like I was in trouble. I tried to find a verbal save.

"No, I mean. . ." But before I was done she smiled to let me know that, once again, she was just messing with me. For some reason I hadn't picked up her patterns yet, so my default setting was to believe everything she told me, but I was starting to see that she liked to keep me on my toes and make me a little uncomfortable from time to time.

A few minutes later we pulled into the parking lot by the rocks, two school truants on the run from the fake high school authorities, basking in the smell of the air as it bounced off of the water. It was another beautiful day, cold but sunny, like the universe knew we would be coming back to our special place again. No amount of crisp blue water, or fresh air, or beautifully positioned stones in the water could command my attention more than she did. *Sorry nature, you know I love you, but you just don't compare to Annalise.*

We parked and made our way back down to those stones, and after a few tenuous steps we were in the middle of them, surrounded on either side by water and wind. It was like a scene from one of those old films where everything is heightened by the environment; all that was missing was the crescendo of an academy-award winning score in the background. It played in my mind, if not in reality.

What was unmistakably real was Annalise; her black hair tossing about her face as she stood to my left; the bundle of her coat as it clutched her body underneath, keeping it warm from the breeze. I was of course freezing again, but I hardly noticed. I felt the sensation in my ears the most, they were always the part of my body that was least friendly with any sort of cold, but I refused to wear hats because I looked like an idiot in hats. I felt the tingle begin to intensify, but I felt no pain at all. Once I found my footing on the lopsided stone beneath me, I distributed my weight firmly between my feet, this time they were covered by shoes that could grip the terrain underneath.

To my left Annalise stood gazing as she did, and for a brief moment I looked off to my right, and as I did I absorbed the scenery that decorated the horizon. It was nothing short of stunning. When I shifted my weight back I almost didn't realize that I was engaged in one of Annalise's ninja-attack kisses, but my arms found their place wrapped around her waist, as the puff of her coat thinned when she pressed into my body.

As we kissed I split in two, with half of me engaged in a kiss that truly belonged in the annals of historic kisses (there was no such thing, but there should have been, and had there been this would have easily made the top three). The other part of me was experiencing the entire moment from a distance; detached from my body in a way that allowed me to experience it like I was watching a film of us. I thought about all sorts of things in those few seconds; I thought that for the first time in my life my 5'8" frame felt every bit of 6'8", as I angled my head downwards to kiss her. It wasn't just an issue of physics and math that made me feel that way, she made me feel bigger than I was in every way imaginable.

I felt that wind again, intense even on a nice day like this one, gusting against our bodies aggressively. The tingling that I felt a minute ago was replaced by a sensation that I would normally call pain, but I couldn't feel any pain while I was kissing her, my body simply wouldn't register it. That physiology thing again, you know? In the hierarchy of sensations, the feeling of her lips against mine trumped any pain the body could possibly imagine. When she pulled away my Annalise drug wore off, and almost immediately that intellectual pain became actual pain. "You're a potato," she said to me, and my cheeks shot up towards my eyes. It was the oddest and most wonderful thing I'd ever heard. I had no idea what it meant, but I knew that I liked it when she said it to me.

"I'll be a potato if you want me to be," I joked back, holding her close to me in the gusting wind.

"It's not what I want you to be, it's what you are."

"Are you ever going to tell me what that means?"

"Maybe," she said. "If you're lucky. But then again, you may never know."

"But it does mean something?"

"Uh-huh."

"Okay. Then I'll try to figure it out."

"You can try," she said, smiling. "But you'll never really know."

The bridge in the distance formed a metal horizon line, floating over the water as hundreds of cars sped over it, on their way to no one knew where. They looked like little dots to me, and as I watched them I thought about how little those dots knew of this place. Most of them probably made that trip every morning, speeding by with eyes facing forward and coffee cups filling their hands. This was just another day for them. They drove by in their masses, perhaps not even glancing to their right to see what must look to them like a single line of tiny little stones, carving a strip through the water. They had no idea what they drove over every day, but we knew, didn't we, Annalise?

Squatting down on the rocks, the breeze decided to relax itself, and my ears were thankful to feel blood flowing through them again. When the wind calmed into nonexistence, I could appreciate the view even more; it was as beautiful as always. Inside I was as calm as the wind, so I decided it was a perfect time to discuss what I really didn't want to discuss. "So," I began. "When are you leaving for Peru?"

"I'm leaving next week, and I'll be back after the holidays." It was mid-December. Even though it was cold at the rocks, the general weather had stayed unseasonably warm, and until she mentioned the holidays I had almost forgotten the time of year. She was going to be gone for two weeks. Two. Damn. Weeks. "Oh, that's cool," I lied. Don't really know why I even bothered, because I could see on her face that she read my bullshit as if it was written on my lying forehead. Her right eyebrow shot up to the sky in a look of disapproval that scared me a little. She saw that something was wrong, but she couldn't see all the way inside of me. I still had my walls up just like she did. We both had a side business of wall building.

But the truth I was trying to hide was that the idea of her leaving devastated me in ways that defied typical means of explanation. There wasn't an easy comparison I could make because nothing standard compared. I was a sensitive kid and shit like that hit me hard. The rational part of me knew that she was just taking a short vacation with her family, but she might as well have told me she was leaving and never coming back. I don't know why I reacted that way. Maybe it was insecurity, or maybe I was just done with people leaving me for any period of time. Who knows, but what I can tell you was that her news birthed a chasm in me, a deep and palpable abyss that I couldn't see the bottom of, no matter how much I peered over the edge and squinted. This was all very dramatic, I know. More heightened teenaged emotion, right? Right. But my pain was so real in that moment that I could scarcely fathom the true nature of its existence.

In my messed up mind she was leaving and never coming back, and I would be left with only my memories:

of recollections, of yearning, of surprise emails and late night texts, and, of course, of her sweet kisses. All those thoughts unfolded in seconds, the emotions a series of dominos, falling in such synchronized rapidity that it was impossible to tell which came first; which was cause and which was effect. It didn't matter; it all just became sadness in the end.

"Logan," she called out to me. I had been staring without realizing that I was doing so. Lost in thought, as they say, only I was lost in more than thought, I was just plain lost.

"Yeah, sorry," I snapped back, doing my absolute worst at attempting to sound normal. "I was just. . ." I trailed off. "I'm just a little sad that you're leaving. We were just getting started." It was as honest as I could be. I didn't know how she would react, but it almost didn't matter. I had no choice but to let her see me as I really was in that moment.

"I'm sad, too, actually," she said. "I feel the same as you do. This is special, you and me, and I really don't want to leave right now, but I have to go see my family. We do it every year."

"I know, I understand. I was just worried, like, you wouldn't come back, or you'd forget about me. You know, you'd meet some tall handsome Peruvian guy named Juan or something, and forget all about our time here at the rocks. Peru has rocks, too, right?" I was so insecure, but my insecurity was only acceptable when paired with my vulnerability, because I was under the false belief that the only way to prevent my worst fears was to name them out loud, however crazy they sounded. Annalise looked down and gave me her love-grin.

"Yeah, there are rocks in Peru," she answered. "Lots of rocks, and beaches, and beautiful places with handsome men. And yeah, I'm sure that some of them are even named Juan." As she spoke those words my heart sank. "But," she continued. "Those rocks aren't these rocks, and those guys aren't you. I don't want them, I want you." Our eyes met in that moment and the look in hers spoke to me in ways that her mouth never could; I would have been hard pressed to ascribe an adjective to that look as it wasn't just loving, or beautiful, or even romantic. It was something I didn't have the words to describe, and yet I understood it entirely.

"Thank you," I said. I don't know why I said those particular words, or even what they meant in that context, but they made sense to me to say. I leaned over and kissed her. What else could I do in that moment? I felt connected to her, and highly vulnerable, and still a little bit sad, despite her reassurances, but there was nothing else I could do except tell the insecure voice in my head to shut the hell up, and just experience that moment for what it was.

After the rocks, Anna and I spent the early afternoon together. I took her to lunch at the same diner Pete had embarrassed the hell out of me in the other day. I introduced her to their killer coffee, and she introduced me to the existential questions of life.

"So I decided to finish my senior year," she said.

"I remember from our text the other night. I think that's a great idea. I'm glad you came to that conclusion."

"It wasn't that I thought I couldn't finish, you know. It wasn't that at all. I know I can get through some dumb math and science classes. It's just that. . ."

"What?" I asked.

"It's just that things are really hard at home, and I don't have time to do projects or homework after school, and I sure as hell don't have time to study. I'm tired all the time. Plus I have a lot of responsibilities."

Responsibilities. That word and I were tight, like two kids who were forced to be friends because their parents were friends, but they really hated each other and just hung out out of habit. "I know all about that," I said. "When my dad left I had to become, like, the man of the house. I'm used to it now, but it was really rough at first. I went from doing almost nothing to doing everything because my mom can't."

"Like what kind of stuff?" she asked me softly.

"Cooking, cleaning, shopping, driving her to therapy, picking up her prescriptions, doing laundry, everything."

"Shit," she said. "That's a lot. I do a lot of that, too.

"Yeah," I agreed. "It feels like a lot sometimes."

She looked up and thought for a moment, like she was trying to choose just the right words. "Well think of it this way, you're practicing."

"Huh?"

"You're practicing. In fact, if you think about it, you're kind of lucky."

"Lucky?" That was an adjective I never would have paired with my life at the time. "What do you mean?"

"Well, the way I see it, you can't control your parents' marriage, and you sure as hell can't control your mom's issues, right?"

"Right," I agreed, still not knowing where she was going with this.

"But all of the things you've had to do after he left, those aren't bad things, are they? They're the things that we all have to learn how to do at some point in our lives anyhow, right? You're just getting some early, on the job training so you'll be more prepared later on in life. Seems lucky to me."

I'd never thought it that way. Of course I hadn't. Of course it took Anna to make me look on the bright side of things, even if I still hated having to be a seventeen year old adult. "That's a new way of looking at it. I guess you're right."

"Why thank you," she said, smiling. She looked so beautiful that I sometimes lost my train of thought when I was talking to her. She wasn't hot. Hot was cheap. Hot was ordinary. She was beautiful in a way that no other girl I'd ever met was. Her beauty created futures in my mind; landscapes of possibilities that were waiting to be filled with dates, people, memories, houses, and the little beautiful babies Annalise just had to have one day, because how could her babies not be beautiful?

"No, thank you. Leave it to you to look on the bright side."

"So are you a good cook?" she asked.

Now that was indeed a loaded question. The short answer, the one that would have just garnered me a quick and impressive smile, hug, and maybe another kiss would have been:

Yes, I'm an undiscovered talent in the culinary world, a diamond in the rough as they say. Right now I'm only making pork chops and mashed potatoes for my mom, but once those in the industry know of my particular gastronomic prowess, I'm gonna light the world on fire and win numerous James Beard awards like those dudes on Top Chef, thanks for asking.

Now even though such bravado was totally out of character, it was the kind of thing I'd have liked to have been able to profess in order to impress a girl who had me wishing I was more than I was, but at the same time I was no liar, and to say any two syllables of that elegant bullshit would have been toxic to what I was trying to do. So I went with the tepid truth of the matter.

"I'm alright, I won't be appearing on any TV shows,

but I can avoid messing food up with the best in the world."

"Don't sell yourself short, I bet you can cook your ass off."

So here was the truth. I could cook my ass off, but it had taken a long and winding road to get there. I'd dabbled in cooking when I was kid, it always interested me, but my interest waned when I realized that there were things I could better spend my time doing, like reading comics and playing video games with Pete. After that, chopping onions and making sauces took a back seat to all things electronic or Marvel-related. I still loved the idea, but it took the dissolution of my previously perfect, nuclear family for me to really cut my teeth in the kitchen.

Once I had to be our household cook I had to make sure that shit wasn't disgusting or harmful. I took to the teacher of us all, YouTube, and I learned some basic stuff that your average medieval peasant worried about contracting the Black Death probably knew more about than me. Cooking temperatures, knife skills, how to rest meat, all of it. Those things would have been like some bizarre alien language to me had you said them to me before my Dad walked out the front door, never to return. But now? Now I had some skills in the kitchen, but I didn't want to brag to impress a girl, even Annalise.

"I'm getting better since I have to cook all the time."

"Well maybe one day you can cook for me." I probably looked hilarious trying to stay cool when she said that to me, my face struggling to maintain its cool exterior while I low key tried to keep my heart from beating its way straight into a panic attack.

"I'd be honored, are you kidding? But I'd need to know what kind of food you like before I could really make you something good."

"Can you make Spanish food?"

Oh no. Here it came. "Nah, I'm fake Spanish, I'm sorry."

Anna almost spit out the sip of coffee she'd just taken. "I'm sorry, you're what?"

"Fake Spanish. Oh shit, I'm sorry, have you never met one of me before?"

"What are you saying right now," she asked, laughing as she did.

"Oh, we've never talked about this, have we? Okay, time to do this right here and now, are you ready?" She nodded, fighting the smiles back. "Well, I know that I sound Spanish as shit with the last name I have, but I'm a fake Spanish person."

Anna almost fell over laughing, but she played my little silly game for fun. "Okay, I'll bite. A fake Spanish person?"

"That's right, pleased to meet you. If you've never met one of us before I'm happy to be your first."

"So what makes you fake, exactly?"

"Well that's a complicated question, but I guess the most egregious example of my fake Spanish-ness would be my inability to say or understand a damn word outside of 'hola' and 'gracias' which, as you can hear, I can't even say right."

"Okay, I'm starting to get the picture," she joked. "What else?"

"Let me see, there's so much, where do I start. My grandfather, who I never met btw, was from Puerto Rico, but I've never been. My mom speaks Spanish fluently but I can't say anything right. What else? Well, I can't cook Spanish food at all. Not that I can't, exactly, but I never have. I eat and cook like a white boy—my Dad's genes expressing themselves in his absence so that I have a memory of the man one day. I don't even like spice that much."

"Me either!" she yelled.

"Wait, you're Peruvian, correct? You're real Spanish."

"Half Peruvian, if that's even a thing. Now that I think about it that sounds dumb. My mom's from Peru and my equally absent dad was Mexican, from what I hear anyhow."

"What you hear?"

"Never met the man. He got my mom pregnant eighteen years ago and split to God-Knows-Where. He's probably there now with more illegitimate Mexican babies than he can count."

"That sucks about your dad, I'm sorry," I said.

"Ditto."

"But enough about those losers, back to what I was saying."

"Right, I'm sorry, I didn't mean to interrupt."

"Where were we? I lost track. It's hard to keep all of my fake characteristics straight, you know. Right! Can't speak, can't cook, can't dance."

"Woah, woah, woah," she said. "Can't dance? I can forgive the speaking and the cooking, but no dancing?"

"Not like a good Spanish boy should be able to, no. I'm afraid not. You?"

"It's like my favorite thing to do. I love parties just for the dancing."

"I can't say the same."

"Okay, I agree, you are fake Spanish. I'll have to show you our ways."

"I know, I admit it freely. I understand if you wanna break things off now."

"Shut up," she said, grabbing my cheeks and kissing

me gently. "Fine, I can live without the dancing, but I would like you to cook something for me."

"What do you like?"

"Steak," she said definitively.

"Steak, got it. What else?"

"More steak. Seriously, I love it."

"You just like steak? What about chicken or pork?" I asked, fascinated by her weird eating habits.

"Nah, I'm good without all that. Gimme steak and I'm a happy girl."

Suddenly a flashbulb went off. Flickering though it may have been it was still an idea. "How about you let me take you out on a real date. To a restaurant. I'll make sure they serve steak, I promise."

"Yeah?"

"Yeah," I said back. "I love our time here, but let me take you on a proper date. Actually, there's a really good steak house a few towns over, you wanna go?"

"Hell yeah, I wanna go," she said back.

"Wow. I just asked Annalise out."

"What?"

I realized that I'd let some inner dialogue become a little to external right then, so I pulled back. "Sorry," I said. "I'm just happy to be here with you. And I'm happy to eat steak with you also."

"I'm happy to eat steak too."

"And being here with me?"

"Eh," she joked. "I mean, I'm not mad about that. But that steak though. . ."

This time I kissed her. It was impulsive and it was real, but it was the first time that I kissed her first. I realized this last time she kissed me, and while I was happy any time my lips were pressed against hers, it was my turn to take charge and show her just how I felt about her. She seemed surprised, but then her hand came up and touched my face, and her fingers danced over the back of my head. They felt like warmth, they felt in their gentle embrace like they had the power to shut everything that worried me off, and replace those feelings with the promise of a better tomorrow. I separated, smiling at her, and waiting for her to react in some way. "So, when are we getting that steak?"

It wasn't the reaction I was hoping for. I was hoping for her to faint, her body's natural reaction to the amount of passion I brought to my kissing game, but strangely that didn't happen.

"When do you leave?"

"Soon," she said, and my heart dropped.

"Well, then how about tonight?" That sounded perfect to me.

After the rocks and lunch I drove Anna home and headed back to my place for a little before going out for dinner. When I got home it was late afternoon. I had a little time before steak, so I decided to change and relax for a while. Inside I found Mom watching TV in her chair, as per usual. "Hey there," she said as I walked in, which was weird because sometimes she didn't even notice if I came or went, let alone acknowledge me. "I'm glad you're home."

"Me too." That was a lie. I felt like the worst son in the world for saying that, but telling the truth would have been worse. Nonetheless she seemed to be having a good evening. "I'm gonna grab dinner with Pete tonight if that's okay," I told her. "I'll order you a pizza before I go if that's cool."

"Don't worry," she said. "I can order it. Tell him I said hi, okay?"

"Okay. I'm not leaving yet, I'm gonna go upstairs for a while and take a shower. That okay?"

"Of course it is. You don't have to ask me if every-thing's okay, you know. I'm good here with my shows."

"Okay, Mom. Thanks."

"Just make sure to say goodbye on your way out in case I'm asleep when you get home."

"Do you have all your meds ready?" I asked.

"Yeah. This new one makes me really groggy. I wish they'd find one that worked without all of the side effects."

"They will, Mom," I said. "They will. I love you."

"I love you too, baby. Have fun, okay?"

"I will."

Upstairs I hung out for a bit. It was earlier than I would have done this on any other day, but I made my way into the bathroom and climbed into the tub. I took my usual spot, only this time it wasn't to pray or wish. One of my two greatest wishes had already happened, finally, and I wasn't about to be redundant with the universe.

My rookie mistake was leaving the bathroom door slightly ajar, enough that Mom, who I mistakenly thought was passed out on the couch, pushed in thinking that it was unoccupied. "Oh, I'm sorry," she said, probably thinking that I was taking a shower. I wasn't. And the look on her face as I stood, fully dressed in our bathtub was both hilar-ious and kind of horrifying at the same time. "What are you doing?" she asked me. No doubt I looked shady as hell, like I was the cat, and the canary had just fled for its little life out of our window.

"Nothing," I said, trying in vain to play it off all cool. She saw right through me like any mom would have. "Just catching some fresh air."

"What's wrong with the windows in your room?"

"Nothing," I answered back quickly, trying to secure a plausible lie in my head as I spoke. "I was just in here already so I figured I'd take a few deep breaths, you know?"

Mom looked at my dumb ass sideways, and it was one of those true parent-kid moments where she took pity on my sorry excuse for a lie and let me keep up the facade. "Just let me know when you're done getting air because I need to go to the bathroom, okay?"

"Okay, Mom, I will."

She closed the door behind her and left me to my ritual. My heart was still beating a little fast from her having walked in on me, but it was starting to slow. Like I said, I wasn't there to wish. For once, something I'd wanted maybe more than anything had come to me, and I only had one thing to say to whoever was listening before I went to cook dinner for us.

"Thank you," I whispered to the universe. "Just, thank you."

SIX

Where I learn that food and Annalise just didn't get along, and where she struggles to pronounce types of steak correctly.

So I finally got Anna to agree to go on a proper date with me. Well, I guess *proper* was the wrong word. Proper would have been ringing her doorbell dressed in my finest, smiling at her mom and saying something like "*Hi, nice to meet you Ms., I'm Logan. Yeah, Puerto Rican actually but no, I don't speak it, sorry. I'm here to take your daughter out to eat steak because, well, that seems to be the only food she wants to eat. Yes, I agree, that's a little weird, but ladies' choice, you know? I promise I'll have her back before curfew and, yes, my intentions are pure and of course I wanna be a doctor or lawyer one day. Cool? Cool. Nice meeting you Ms. Annalise.*" So not totally proper I guess, but also not the all-night texting and making out in cars stuff that had formed the basis of our relationship up to that point. It was time to go out for real. Tables, waitresses, me paying for things, of course, and I couldn't have been more excited about it.

The only barrier to our first real date was Annalise's prohibition on all normal food. Seriously, the girl was the mortal enemy of all regular forms of sustenance. Now, for all of her otherworldly Goddessness and otherwise amazing personal qualities, the girl didn't eat shit—like nothing. She hated all food that Man had yet invented. She had some things in particular that triggered her gag reflex hard, but there was a whole hierarchy of stuff she just generally didn't mess with. Unfortunately for me, that list included almost all food on planet Earth. On a scale of 1-5, with 1 being *I slightly dislike this*, and 5 being *get that disgusting shit out of my visual field before I vomit on your shoes*, Annalise's 'favorites' included:

Soup. The girl hated soup. She hated soup like most people hated poverty, genocide, and injustice. She hated soup the way most people would hate the idea of roaches crawling in and out of their ears while they sleep. I know it sounds strange, and it was. And it wasn't just a certain kind of soup, either. Her discrimination knew no boundaries. If you could puree a series of ingredients with an immersion blender and serve it in a bowl, it was evil to Annalise. It was so bad that the mere suggestion of any sort of soup would inspire a dramatic fake-barf and an eye roll that signified what a dumb fucking suggestion you had just made to her. When I asked her why, she told me that her mom had made soup for her and her sisters all the time as a child, and forced them to eat it no matter whether they liked it or not. That explanation also covered a more minor culinary hatred–milk. Just see the explanation above, it's the same story.

Spicy food. Now, when I say 'spicy', you're probably thinking of some Sriracha-slathered, Ghost chili type-shit, right? Like some craziness of a dish that would leave your taste buds numb and your stomach a hostile environment for weeks. Nah, nothing of the sort. I mean, sure, she wouldn't even consider something like what I just described. Not to sound racist, but I never in my life met a

Hispanic girl who didn't like at least some spice in their food. She was the one. She might have been the only one.

So, what did she like to eat? Steak. The girl loved steak. She loved it so much that it was the only type of restaurant that she would go to, sight unseen, which is how we ended up a steak-place for our first official date (not proper, mind you, but official). Not that I disagreed, steak was great, but still. That night I had the duel pleasure of Annalise's company and a juicy 16 oz., bone-in ribeye to boot. Win-win right there. That steak alone would have illuminated the darkest of nights, but its meaty power was magnified tenfold while eating it across the table from my Anna.

She kept those baby browns fixed hard on the double sided plastic menus with the delectable cuts of dead cow all over them. When the waiter came over Anna went mute. It was the weirdest thing. She first motioned to me to order, so I got my bone-in rib eye. *Yes, I said 16 ounces. Medium-rare, what else? Steak fries, sure.* When it was Anna's turn she held the menu across the table, like she wanted to show me something. She turned it around so the writing was facing me, and pointed to the steak on the bottom, right hand side. *I want that*, she mouthed to me.

Ummm, I said, *she's gonna have the sirloin and shrimp combo. Medium-well. 10 ounce or 8 ounce? 8 of course, small salad—no tomatoes, cause ew—and none of that bitter purple stuff. Thank you.* When the waiter walked away I shot Anna a *what the hell* face. I knew something was up when she was so passive, and she told me that she couldn't say the word sirloin. Literally. Bullshit, I said playfully. You speak the fastest Spanish known to man and you can't say SIRLOYN? She gave me that frustrated smile of hers.

"I just can't say that word good," she told me. "Don't make fun of me."

"I'm not. It's just funny."

"Shut up," she joked.

She didn't have to say sirloin if she didn't want to. She didn't have to say anything at all. Just sit there and make me forget that there's anything bad in this world, and I'll pronounce your cuts of steak forever, okay? Deal. We made small talk while waiting for our unpronounceable food—a laugh here and there, a bit of teenaged gossip—*wait, Mr. A is sleeping with who now? James got suspended for doing what in the teacher's cafeteria?* We talked and ate, ate and talked, and the more words we exchanged the closer to her I felt. Looking back on it now, I'm confident in saying that Annalise was probably the most observant person I ever encountered, but I had my moments, too. I saw the little things.

For example, while we were eating she left her shrimp skewer for last, and cut her meat like a left handed person (knife in left, fork in right), even though she was a righty. She looked down almost the entire time she ate, with occasional sideways glances towards the floor, and looking up at me only when I was saying something important. Sometimes a grin, sometimes a full smile. *What is it*, I'd ask. She didn't answer, only shook her head like *no, I'm not verbalizing the things in my head right now, try again later*, while smiling even deeper. When I pushed she told me that she was having Happy Thoughts, and when she said that, I didn't pry any further because I wanted to believe that those Happy Thoughts were about us.

We were both tired from our epic series of micro-dates, and after we finished our steaks and talked for a while I paid the bill and it was time to take her home. Outside the moonlight bounced off of Anna's face, and in it I saw her in a whole new way. It was a flashbulb moment, burned into my memory to this day. It's funny how memory worked like that, isn't it? The most common of moments, the most pedestrian of things, can sometimes be one of the handful of moments that you could recall to your dying day like it had just happened. Anna's face in the moonlight was one of those moments for me. It wasn't anything special if you'd been watching from the outside. Just two kids on a date about to get in a car. Nothing unusual. But for me it was everything. Before we got in the car we stood looking at the passing traffic. "So how was that?" I asked.

"The steak? A little overdone but really good."

"No, not the steak. The date. How did I do?"

"You want me to rate your performance?"

"Something like that," I said.

"Okay, then I give you a 9 out of 10."

"A 9!"

"Oh, I see," she said. "You wanted to be perfect?"

"Well, kinda, yeah. What did I do wrong?"

"You see, that's where you went wrong. Sometimes you just have to let perfection be without seeing how many likes and comments it gets. Just let perfection speak for itself."

"Wait, let me get this straight. You had me at 10 until I asked you to rate my performance, and then I got downgraded to a 9?"

"Exactly," she said, that devious grin finding its way across her face. "Let perfection be perfection, or it ceases to be perfection."

"Damn, that was poetic, you should write that down."

"I did," she said, smiling. "I wrote it in my journal."

"You journal?"

"I've never used that word as a verb before. I kinda like it. And yeah, I journal, I guess. Let's get in the car it's getting chilly."

She was right, the wind was picking up and it was

starting to feel like the holidays. Not only had the air taken on a chill, stores were starting to look like Christmas had thrown up all over them. Lights, red and green, fake Christmas trees in stores, all that holiday cheer stuff. I had my own reason to celebrate, and she was sitting across from me, looking heartbreakingly beautiful. "Now take me home, I wanna sleep so bad!"

"I'm exhausted too," I said.

"Are you saying I'm exhausting?"

"Exactly," I joked.

"Well this date just got downgraded to an 8. Maybe a 7 if you keep talking."

We smiled at each other and then I drove her home. In a few days she'd be gone, off to the motherland, and I was already quietly freaking out about it. I tried to hide it as best I could, but I suspected that I was failing miserably.

"Look, about Peru," she began. My whole body tensed up. "I don't want you to worry, okay. I know it's early in our relationship to up and leave, but we go every year, and it's just to see family, not to be with all the Juan's. I promise you."

"You didn't have to say that," I told her. "But thanks for saying it anyhow. I'm gonna miss you."

"Potato."

"Potato," I answered, thinking it was like a cute thing we said to one another. I was wrong.

"Still no, it's my word, remember?"

"Right, how could I forget? My mistake."

"You're forgiven, don't worry."

She leaned in one last time for one more kiss, and it was the definition of bittersweet. After I dropped her off I headed home. I was exhausted, too. It had been a long and wonderful day, but I needed to sleep also. When I got home Mom was asleep, and there was a note telling me that there was leftover pizza in the fridge if I wanted any. It was sweet, but the thought of any more food was nauseating to me, so I skipped the cold pizza and went up to my room. For the first time in a while, I was content, and closing my eyes to go to sleep was something I looked forward to, because I knew what I'd dream about.

Part Two

———————

WHERE ANNALISE FLIES TO THE
MOTHERLAND TO HANG OUT ON SOME
PERUVIAN BEACHES, I EARN THE MONIKER
PETTY CROCKER, AND I LEARN THAT LOVE
CAN'T BE RANKED ON THE SAME SCALE AS
DATES CAN.

"So come on let it go
Just let it be
Why don't you be you
And I'll be me."

James Bay, *Let it Go*.

"She was the kind of girlfriend God gives you young, so
you'll know loss the rest of your life."
Junot Diaz, *The Brief Wondrous Life of Oscar Wao*

...I could never stop thinking that maybe she loved
mysteries so much that she became one.
---John Green, *Paper Towns*

Interlude

HERE

Here is our geography, the limitations and opportunities placed on us by our environment, represented with a capital H because it's always a proper noun for us. Our town, our state, our neighborhood. Scale doesn't matter.

Here is where Our Story takes place, but then again, it's where every story takes place. It's the location where your life is magnetized to either repel or attract, and that's a choice we make, or is made for us. Some of us stay because the pull of familiarity is too great to resist, while others feel the push at a young age, like a hurricane level gust of wind propelling them the hell out of Dodge. Some only think that they want out, and maybe they do, but when the reality of There sets in, they run back as fast as their feet will carry them.

SEVEN

Where I learn that love can't be accurately ranked on a scale of 1-10.

I woke up on the morning of her departure sincerely hopeful that Peru had vanished from the world map while I'd slept. I didn't care about the particular source of its destruction, mind you, only that the entire country was now a memory for the geography textbooks of tomorrow. Maybe it was an invasion by a hostile, South American neighbor (there were always feuds over this border or that national export), or maybe some sort of Hiroshima-like atomic event had taken place in order to settle a long, bloody ground war that raged on just a little too long while the rest of the world proceeded unaware. It didn't matter to me, so long as the political borders of our neighbors to the south had been promptly and inalterably changed to eliminate Peru from being a place my Annalise could disappear to.

I wasn't worldly, but for some reason my far flung hypotheses involving Peru's geopolitical obliteration didn't seem as crazy as all that. After all, I was pretty sure that we in the good-old Northern part of the continent were bliss-fully ignorant of the woes of our southern neighbors. Most of us didn't know anything about the counties that actually bordered us on either end. South of Mexico might as well have been another universe; I would have been hard pressed to name a political party, a head of state, a national dish, or a major export of any country in Latin America, so the idea that an unknown Peruvian civil war had come to a swift, late night end with some sort of nuclear device, didn't seem so far out of the realm of possibilities.

I checked the news feed on my phone, feeling somewhat sociopathic that I was actively hoping for the destruction of an entire country just to keep my (could I have called her my girlfriend at that point?). . . closer to me. But I suppose I knew that it was unlikely to see the headline "Former South American country decimated in the early morning, map being redrawn for schoolchildren" adorning any front pages.

What I did have on my phone was a good morning text from Annalise.

Morning. I actually slept last night. Must have been all the steak. I love Peru but hate leaving you for this long. Don't worry. No Juan's. I'll text you when I land.

She'd kept to her word that she'd text me before getting on the plane, the wheels of which had left the ground about two hours before I had woken up. The text was nice, but it hardly replaced the comfort I normally would have enjoyed knowing that I'd see her in person, but it was all I had. There was no bringing her back, and according to all available social media news sources, Peru had not met the war-like, destructive end that I had hoped for, so instead of more horizontal pining, I decided that getting up and being at least semi-productive was a better idea.

It's in moments like that one when the *Bleh* appeared, ready to hang out like that dirt bag friend who invites himself over, cleans out your fridge, and then stays around way past the lengths of social acceptability. It took a hold of me, and my attempts to be a productive citizen were undermined by the paralysis of my mind. I wasn't egocentric, I knew that I was just one of thousands—probably hundreds of thousands—of other teens going through pretty much the same thing. Hell, in a weird way I was happy for once to have normal problems, but I was also a rookie at that game, and my inexperience was showing itself.

But the one thing I knew how to do was move ahead when I was mentally injured. It was what I was best at. We all had family problems, and girl trouble, and stress about school. My feelings weren't exceptional in any way. I was going to drive into school with Pete today. I picked him up at his house looking despondent as hell, and he already knew what was up. "Peru still there?"

"Yeah, nothing on my news feed about its annihilation. Sucks."

"Does it?" he asked, a little disgusted with me. "I think there's something seriously wrong with you."

"Well I could have told you that already. But why, specifically?"

"Why?" he asked, raising his eyebrow at me. "Let's take a moment to analyze. I get being into a girl, trust me, but I've never wished for the destruction of an entire culture just so I could keep that girl domestic. That's nuts."

"Yeah, I know. I don't really want that, obviously."

"But if you were in the same situation and simultaneously the totalitarian head of some rouge state with nuclear capabilities?"

"I probably would have pressed that little red button about 4am last night."

"You're sick."

"Also no secret. In all fairness to the Peruvian people I would have sent a diplomatic telegram warning them of their impending destruction from the hellfire of the good old U.S. of A if they allowed Anna's flight into their airspace. I'm sure they would have conceded before anyone was actually incinerated. I mean, who would take the complete destruction of their country to allow one American girl in for a Christmas vacation? No responsible leader I know of."

"Again," Pete said, looking at me seriously. "Let me reiterate. You're a sick little puppy who's obsessing over this girl."

Maybe Pete was right. Maybe I was a little obsessive. But then again, she was my first real girlfriend (I'd started calling her this in my head even though we'd never designated any official titles, but maybe that was me obsessing again). This was my first rodeo, so maybe a little obsessing was in order.

School was school, only I was locked up in in-school suspension for the better part of the day, with two more days of student incarceration to follow. I knew I wasn't supposed to be enjoying my time in there, but the fact of the matter is that I didn't have to deal with anyone's crap. No annoying kids, no more teachers' dirty looks, nothing but my lonesome, some assignments, and time to think. Truth was I would have very much preferred to spend the rest of my high school career locked up in in-school suspension, but that just wasn't in the cards.

They really did try to treat it like a prison. They'd escort me to the bathroom when I had to go, and walk me to the lunch room with a security guard like I was on some

Hannibal-Lecter type shit. It was ridiculous, but it did make me feel way cooler than I was in reality. After 9 periods of that silliness the first day of my sentence was over, and I was a free man. I was still thinking about Annalise, of course, so Pete and I decided to go to the guru of all things involving females our age: Jason.

There was a Jason in every high school in America, and probably internationally, too. You probably knew a Jason or two when you were a kid. He was that dude in high school who always got girls, even though doing so violated every natural law of the universe. Kid was ugly as hell. Nerdy too, but not comic nerdy like me. N-E-R-D-Y, like Dungeons & Dragons shit. He was also shorter than should have been acceptable in a male at our age, I towered over the kid like I was a giant, yet he had girls around him like those hippos in Africa that have birds living on their backs. He was never without a girlfriend, and if one dared to break up with him there was a long line of contenders waiting to fill her spot. I wouldn't say we were friends, but we were cool enough with each other for the occasional hang out, mostly to pick his brain on just how the hell he managed to acquire such strong female attention.

His only distinction, besides his ability to convince even the hottest of girls that he was worthy of their time, happened in fourth grade when he got hit by a car. No joke. Smushed. Broken everything. Settlement lawsuit that would pay for a full ride to Dartmouth had he possessed the necessary intelligence to get in to such a prestigious institution. So here's what happened. Jason loved soccer. I couldn't emphasize this enough. The World Cup was his Olympics; had he been born in the UK rather than New York he would have been one of those hooligans who start fires and attack people in the stands when their team loses.

As it was he was just a kid who was really into soccer, which he of course refused to call soccer. *Futbol*, he'd say in a fake Hispanic accent (faker than mine), *I'm watching Futbol*. Shit drove me nuts.

So anyhow, one day he's on the field for recess in sixth grade and he's kicking the ball around with some friends. All of a sudden a kick that was a little too vigorous by our Guatemalan exchange student sent the ball off the field into the adjacent, teacher's parking lot. Now the intelligent thing would have been to cast a glance left or right before diving after the ball, but Jason was an impulsive tweenager, and that dude leapt into teacher car traffic like his team's victory in the World Cup depended on it. Had he looked he might have observed Mr. Sullivan, our science teacher, barreling off for his lunch break way too fast. But as history actually went, Jason neglected that age old lesson on looking both ways and the rest was a long recovery in the hospital. Now I was sitting with the older version of Jason, hoping like hell he could make me feel better about my girl problems.

"Attention, my friends, it's all about attention." That was always Jason's go-to line about girls. It was his contention that most guys treated girls like objects, so much so that if you could just be a normal human being and listen to them, you'd catch them like a fly trap. Jason loved talking about this subject. I suspected he likewise loved the reputation he got as *that-guy-who-gets-girls* more than he liked the actual girls, but maybe I was just being petty and jealous.

"That makes perfect sense," Pete said. "But we're not actually looking for advice on how to get a girlfriend. We both have girlfriends."

"Even Logan?"

"Screw you," I told him, only half joking.

"Sorry, man, it's just that. . .you know. . .you never, ever have a girlfriend. I guess it was bound to happen sooner or later, right?"

"Right," I said, getting angrier with each syllable out of the kid's mouth.

"So what did you want to talk to me about?"

"Well, speaking of his first girlfriend. . ."

"Wait, who are we talking about, just so I have some context."

"Annalise," I told him. It was hard to keep the smile off my face.

"That weird girl?" Jason asked. Now, at that particular moment I was faced with a strange, nano-second response choice. My impulse was to attack him, either verbally or physically (I hadn't decided yet), but the other part of me —the rational side—decided to talk it out.

"She's not that weird girl," Pete said, interjecting. "Have some respect, dude."

"Sorry, I didn't mean anything. It's just that. . ."

"Yeah I get it. Anyways, now you know who my girl-friend is. Go on."

Annalise did have that reputation. I was aware of it before I even first talked to her. Reputations in high school were like temporary tattoos: easy to get, difficult to remove, and even when you did there was always a little left over on your skin. She was a bit of a lone wolf, a little odd, and she kept a small, tight circle of friends around her. She wasn't part of the mainstream. She was the weird girl, and I was the weird guy who was falling in love with her.

"So, anyway, he's with Annalise now, and the girl just took off for a two week detour to South America with her family and my boy is bummed the hell out."

"Understandable," Jason said.

"You ever deal with this sort of thing?"

"Not exactly. Never had a girl skip the country on me if that's what you mean."

"She didn't skip the country," I yelled. "Have you ever had your girlfriend leave your vicinity for more than a few days?"

"Absolutely," he said. "My last girlfriend went to the Ozarks for a week for a family trip."

"Where the hell are the Ozarks?" I asked.

"Down south, somewhere, I think. I'm really not sure. But what of it?"

"How did you deal? How did you not lose your mind? How did you not spend every waking minute thinking she was with some random dude in the Ozarks doing. . .southern shit."

"Man, you're going through some stuff, huh?"

"Yeah," I told Jason. "First girlfriend, you know? I don't know how to deal with shit like this."

"Now it's starting to make sense. If this is your first rodeo I get where your head's at. But don't stress, man, it'll be easier with the next girl, trust me."

The next girl? Did he say the next girl? His words shook me. I couldn't imagine another girl, or not having Anna in my life, and what he was saying played right into the fears I was already feeling.

"Well, let's just focus on this experience for now," I said. "We don't all have girls orbiting us."

"I don't get it either, dude, I'm not much to look at, I admit it. But like I said, listening is the key." He loved repeating that mantra over and over again. In the future he'd become a self-help guru, one of those life-coach types who wrote a paperback every three months repeating the same recycled advice on how to self-actualize and be the best you possible. "But the best advice I could give you is just to keep busy. Keep your mind off shit. Get a hobby.

Get a dog. Focus on school. No, forget that last thing, school sucks, don't focus on that. But distract yourself somehow."

"That makes sense, thanks. I'll give distraction a try."

"I'm telling you, it works."

It works? Okay, Jason, I thought, *let's just see about that.*

For two long weeks my sad teenaged-ass waited as Annalise walked the colonially invented streets of Lima doing God only knows what. As you can imagine, time dragged on like a slug pulling it's disgusting self across your garden and leaving that weird slime trail on the grass. But I did gain an education of sorts while she was gone. I learned that Peruvian Wi-Fi could be dubious as shit, and that I had to continuously resend my texts over and over, waiting and wondering why it took a solid three hours to get my 'Hey, what's up, how's your day going?' returned to me with a little smile emoji. In my overactive, insecure mind I imagined Annalise taken captive by the South American drug cartels when she got off the plane. I'd seen a show once where the cartels sent their guys to wait for pretty girls at the airports and then pretend to be a car service for the girl's family, only to eventually kidnap the girls, demand a ransom, and then take the girls to jungles where they're forced to work synthesizing drugs or as mules.

In some scenarios Annalise was half naked in the Jungles of Peru making meth. In others, though, she wasn't upset at all. As terrifying as the cartel fantasy was, I knew deep down that it was the inner workings of a fucked up, prone-to-exaggeration mind. But the scenario that recurred the most, the one that really frightened me, had nothing to do with drug cartel fantasies, or crashed planes, or anything so dramatic. The thought that literally kept me up most nights of those two weeks was that Annalise had forgotten about what we had before she left; that she'd met some Peruvian kid who was my South American counter-part, someone from her culture, who could speak her language and grew up in a similar household who would just be...easier to be with than I would. Some kid who wasn't from a messed up family like mine. Did she even want that? I didn't really know the answer at the time, but my sad boy brain yelled the answer over and over to me.

The next two weeks were a mix of good moments, bad moments, and a lot of waiting around. When she was at her family's home Anna had Wi-Fi, and we texted back and forth like normal. When she went out almost anywhere else the Wi-Fi was either dial-up-modem slow, or non-existent. I was happy to be speaking to her at all while she was away with family in another country, but it was in those other moments that my mind started racing with insecurities. A two hour gap between texts was two hours to invent reasons other than Wi-Fi as to why she wasn't writing back, and that never ended well.

On several occasions, after allowing my crazy thoughts to escalate into crazy moods, I found myself inadvertently taking it out on Anna when she would finally return a text. I'd write back one word responses like 'okay' or 'fine', knowing that each was an indicator of the opposite emotion. When she would ask me what was wrong, I'd predictably text 'nothing', and continue down the dark road of immaturity. More than once our conversations devolved into mini-fights, mostly (or entirely) due to me not knowing what to do with my own sadness and insecurity, and acting like a complete tool 'cause I needed attention. Those talks followed a predictable pattern, and we had at least three of them during her trip. After each one I felt absolutely terrible, but I couldn't seem to stop. Each time I felt insecure, or jealous of fictitious Peruvian guys, I would say something petty, or engage in my attention seeking texts. Then we'd argue back and forth, usually with Annalise asking me what the hell was wrong with me, telling me 'bye' when I went a little too far, me apologizing profusely and begging her forgiveness, then us getting back to normal.

It became a predictable but unhealthy series of interactions, and I noticed three things about them:

1. I can be petty as all hell when I feel jealous. I never realized this about myself because there were no girls in my life, really, and therefore, there had been no opportunities for me to act petty and jealous in the past.

2. I didn't like that I kept repeating the aforementioned petty behavior. It escalated so badly that at one point, Annalise christened me *Petty Crocker*.

3. Annalise never gave up on me. This was the most important of the three because this was all happening via text, many countries removed from each other, and it would have been easy as all hell to just cut me off, but she never did.

She got mad at me, for sure, and she would text things that would cut right through me and bring me back to sanity, but she never held a grudge, and things always got back to normal with us. I had never been this deep into a relationship, and I noticed that I wasn't being close to the best version of myself. A year of my life had been spent pining and wanting this girl—that Peruvian goddess of my dreams—and there I was acting like a dick, about to forsake the best thing that had ever happened to me. Whether she held a grudge or not, I knew that I wasn't being myself and that I needed to stop being Petty Crocker.

After my third shameful display, I realized that something needed to be said, something not in the moment of my heightened emotion, something I could plan out. I noticed a pattern developing in myself, one that was grander than my increasing pattern of pettiness. I noticed that the writer in me was awakened by her being in my life; that I could speak most clearly to her when the voice I had inside was allowed to speak. After the third, and last, time I needed to explain myself, but in those moments the words that went from my screen to hers weren't really me. They were some sad teenaged boy retarded version of myself, and Annalise need to hear from the real me. The voice in my head spoke the words, and I typed them as quickly as they came into my head:

I miss you so much, and I don't know what to do with that feeling. Baring my soul has become my new favorite activity when I'm with you, so there are a few things I need to tell you about how it's been with us since you've been in Peru. I get scared when things change, and sometimes I get sarcastic, snotty, and use humor to distract from how I really feel. And yes, I become Petty Crocker. I don't know how to wait for you, and I'm sorry. Please forgive me, because it's only due to how much I care about you.

When I finished I sent it to her and waited. Lord only knew when she'd get it over there, but it didn't matter. I had some errands to run, so I left the house for a while. I was waiting in the overly long pharmacy line when I got Annalise's text. Why was it that whenever I had to pick up mom's anti-depressants there were a line of senile, old people having trouble with their insurance companies in front of me in line? It was a mystery of the universe, yet it seemed to be one of the few certainties in life. Death, taxes, and old people who had misread their prescription drug coverage plan on their policy, who now wanted to argue with the 24 year old pharmacist while I waited anxiously for a text from my Peruvian girlfriend. A vibration in my pocket.

Bearing your soul

She had a style of texting all her own. I'd grown accustomed to it, but every now and then the idiosyncrasies of her phone communications intrigued and frustrated me at the same time. She did that a lot—repeat back a portion of what I had said in a longer piece or text or letter, and never with any punctuation attached—so I never knew if she wanted clarity, or didn't understand what I said, or if she was simply repeating something of interest to her. I never knew which it was, and something told me that she wanted it that way. My typical response was to explain what the phrase meant, as if she didn't know.

Yeah, you know, like telling you all of my deep thoughts and feelings

To which she responded with:

I know what it means

And that would be the end of it. On the few occasions that I asked her why she had repeated my text back to me, she either didn't answer or quickly changed the subject. Then I'd elaborate, because I didn't know if we were having a contentious exchange where I had insulted her by assuming she didn't have a good vocabulary, or if we were having a happy conversation where she was just indicating she liked something I had written, in particular. So, to make sure it was the latter and not the former, I'd usually follow up.

I'm sorry about how I've been. I'm sad and

jealous over nothing, and just being stupid. I really, really miss you and I needed to explain that. I really hope that the way I've been hasn't changed anything between us, because I'd hate myself forever for screwing things up with the girl of my dreams.

That was my phrase, not entirely original, but one that I always used when describing her. She was the girl of my dreams—my Peruvian goddess—that girl who the universe delivered to only a select few men in history. The one who rights the wrongs, makes the sun shine through the clouds and who forgives you for being a dick when you text her dumb shit while she's in Peru. You know, that girl.

Girl of your dreams, huh?

This time the punctuation left little to the imagination. My heart did that thing it did when I revealed just a little more than I wanted to, yet somehow felt excited and relieved at the same time. I called her the girl of my dreams, and that carried a particular sort of meaning with it.

Yeah. You are.

There was no point in being coy any more, no point in being shy or holding back. The way I figured it, if I had been honest and raw with my negative emotions, then I needed to be equally honest with my positive emotions. So, there it was, unmistakable, honest, and scary as all hell on my screen and hers.

So, if I ask you something, will you answer me honestly?

I wrote that I would, which was the truth, even if the answer was uncomfortable. And, knowing the preface to her question, it certainly would be.

Like, how strongly do you feel towards me?

And there it was. The question I'd been dreading for a

while. The answer was simple and the answer was timeless. The answer was so clear that I was concerned it would frighten her, so I did my best verbal rope-a-dope to stall. I wrote,

How strongly? Like, how do you want me to answer that?

It was a bad stall, I knew. And Annalise was perceptive enough to know it was a stall. More importantly, she was relentless in getting an answer when she wanted one, so I knew I had about thirty seconds to come up with a proper response before the question got asked over and over again. She wrote,

Okay, how about this...on a scale of 1-10, how strong would you say your feelings are for me?

What? Did she really want me to measure my emotions on a scale like that? It seemed silly at first, and then I remembered this time my dad sliced his hand open after he shattered a drinking glass while washing dishes one night. I volunteered to go to the hospital with him, and I remember seeing a scale on the wall with simply drawn faces—like emojis before there were emojis—ranging from a smiling to a crying face. Each increasingly sad face had a number next to it, and the caption above read *"How severe is your pain?"* I supposed if the medical field used a 1-10 scale to gauge people's injuries then it must have been at least a semi-valid way to measure human emotion. I played along.

Ok, so I want to tell you, but I don't want you to get freaked out if it's higher or lower than you think it should be.

She wrote back,

I don't think it should be anything, I just want you to be honest. And I don't get freaked out about stuff like that, I'm just curious.

She said she wouldn't get freaked out, but I didn't know if I believed her. Even if she did get freaked out, I still had to be honest. The truth was that there was no 1-10 scale to measure how I felt. I was in hopeless, desperate, endless love with Annalise, and no scale, no matter how high it went, could have ever reflected that fact. I figured that starting conservatively was the best way to go, like in a negotiation. I wrote back,

I don't know if I can measure on a scale like that, but definitely a 7.

My heart, which had never really gotten back into a normal rhythm since that conversation started, picked up its unnatural pace even more. Funny how the perception of time could differ so much based on emotion. Between the sending of '7' and Anna's text back, maybe 15 seconds passed, but it seemed like enough time had gone by to elect a new president.

7, huh?

I wrote back,

Ok, like 8 or 9, really.

What the hell was wrong with me? I couldn't stop. Soon I was going to be composing sonnets and declaring my undying love and freaking her the fuck out, no matter what she said. I needed to slow it down.

Oh, 8 or 9? Really? Can I ask you something else, then?

What could she possibly have asked me after that? I was already about to die from all the anxiety. I braced myself. She wrote,

Do you think that you might, you know, love me? Because I get weird with that kind of thing sometimes. It's been said to me before and I didn't know how to react.

The last line couldn't have been more fitting, because I

didn't know how to react at that moment either. I did love her, of course. I think in some ways I always loved her, even before I knew that I did, if that makes any sense. But knowing that you loved someone and using those words were very different things, and I didn't know if I was ready to take the leap while standing in a line at CVS waiting for Mom's meds. Some things—the important things—couldn't be unsaid, and couldn't be written off as a joke. Those were final words; words that defined and changed the nature of things, and I just wasn't ready, emotionally ready, to redefine anything just yet. I thought for a moment before writing back, because I wanted to choose my words carefully.

I don't know exactly how to define how I feel. I don't have a word for it, and it certainly doesn't fit nicely into a whole number on a scale. But what I can tell you is that the sun rises and sets with you, as far as I'm concerned. Talking to you and being with you is the reason I get out of bed in the morning, and you're in my thoughts all day, every day. If you want to define that as love then you can, but that's how I feel. And even if it were love, there are just some things that you don't say through text.

She took a few minutes to write back, and in that time I assumed that she had read between the lines of my text, realized that I loved her hopelessly, and promptly blocked me on her phone, or perhaps changed my name permanently to "Stalker" in her contacts. Either way it felt like an eternity. She finally wrote back,

Potato

I sent back my stock smiley-face emoji, the one that meant everything and nothing all at once. I was still learning the meaning of 'potato', but I knew that it was better than a multitude of other things that she could have responded with. I'd take potato any day of the week, and twice on Sunday. I wrote back,

Potato.

To which she replied, promptly this time,

No. Just no.

I smiled at my screen. She could always make me laugh. I saw the dots in the corner of my phone, and realized that she wasn't done writing. She wasn't as verbose as me—for some reason I could go on and on with really long texts. She could do so much by doing so little. A second text popped up on my screen.

You know, I'm not that special. I'm just an ordinary girl, I'm not sure what all the fuss is about, but I'll take your 8 or 9. And ditto. So I've gotta go, I'm going into the city with Mamita.

I wrote back,

Who's Mamita?

To which she replied,

Oh, it's like grandma. She's taking me shopping in the city. So I'll text you later on, okay?

Ordinary? Did she know what the word meant? Any other girl would have been looking to be contradicted when she said that, looking for someone to step in and sing her praises, but Annalise wasn't like that. The sad part was that I felt like she actually *believed* that she was just another girl. You know, just your run of the mill Peruvian goddess sent to Earth to make me happy.

Ok, text me later.

I heard the annoyed yell of "Next in line," from the obviously disgruntled CVS employee standing in front of me. I was so lost in conversation with Anna that I didn't notice the world-shattering insurance issues of the previous octogenarian had been resolved. I got mom's meds and left, and spent the next few hours at home, relaxing. Mom was having another good day, and we actually hung out and talked a while without anything being weird. It had been some time since that was possible.

After a while I slipped away to my room to do some homework. I thought about my conversation with Annalise from earlier, and I decided that before I went to sleep I needed to be honest with her. I pulled my phone out of my pocket and texted her.

10. And only because you limited me to that. Otherwise it'd be like 15.

She didn't text back, and I didn't expect her to. At that point I'd honestly gotten used to not hearing from her as frequently as I was used to, so I just watched some TV, did some terrible and unnecessary homework, and eventually conked out on my bed. I must have left my phone on ring, because the sound of it going off with a text woke me up. I was disoriented, and looked around the room like I wasn't sure where I was. When I grabbed my phone, I saw it was past midnight, my time, and that Anna had written me back.

At that point in my life I'd been used to bad things. I was good friends with Bad Things, so when good things happened I was almost in paranoid disbelief of their existence. It was a bad habit, but one my life experience had cultivated. That was my reaction as I looked down at my phone. I stared at the words like you stare at something incredible, something that you wouldn't believe was real. On my screen were her words, her magical words. All they said were:

I love you too

EIGHT

Where I ask Anna to accompany me to nerd Heaven.

College was an evil word.

The arbitrary concept that was higher education, became the bane of every upper classman's existence. Parents, teachers, guidance counsellors, even other kids who'd internalized their role in the machine kept reminding you about it. The inquiries on that particular topic came up often and aggressively, and the more you tried to delay their answers in order to just live your life, the more you were reminded of how this *was* your life. Three words came up more often than they should have —*the real world*.

I don't know where the hell this mythological place was —most likely North of Narnia and Southeast of Middle Earth—but apparently we'd all been living in some *Inception*-type dream world for the past seventeen years of our lives. According to all adults, the self-prescribed experts on this topic, this dream world was soon to go the way of Krypton around June of our senior year of high school, after which we'd enter a new, far more real world for which we were apparently underprepared.

Although the general idea of spending another minute in any kind of school made me cringe inside, it was actually Annalise who inspired my getting off my ass and applying. She didn't do this directly, and she was totally unaware that I was even filling out the forms and writing the essays, but the inspiration came from her. She loved when I wrote for her, and I wrote to her often. Little notes that I called love letters; notes on my phone that I'd text her; actual letters I'd send to her house, it didn't matter. Every time she texted a heart emoji, or told me in person how good of a writer I was, she planted a seed of encouragement inside me, and that seed had begun to germinate. I was interested in Boston University because they had this really well known creative writing program, apparently, so I applied there as well as some other places up and down the east coast. I didn't tell anyone, and really, I'm not sure why I was secretive about it, but no one knew. Not Pete, not Mom, and definitely not Anna. In fact, the idea of talking it over with Anna hit a particular nerve.

As we established, I was a relationship virgin, and I'd picked a weird stage of life to jump into the game. From my observations, senior year of high school relationships fell into two distinct and incompatible categories; there were the kids who planned on ending it all the second those tassels were hanging proudly from their graduation caps, and then there were the semi-delusional kids who saw the end of high school as a minor inconvenience in an otherwise unbreakable bond they had with their significant other. I always thought the last group were just stupid, love-struck kids, but when I was in that position myself, the idea of planning to end our relationship—or even the thought of not being with Anna in general—paralyzed me to even think about. So I did what any self-respecting, emotionally immature kid would do with an uncomfortable topic—I went into full denial and pretended none of it was happening. Fingers in ears. La La La La La.

While Anna was off cruising the Motherland I had some time—a lot of it, actually—to contemplate other aspects of my future that were less disturbing to think about. For all his flaws (and let's face it, the kid had many), Jason was absolutely right when he said that I needed a distraction from the sadness that had occupied my mind while she was gone. We stayed in touch, of course, but I tried, despite myself, to have some confidence in our relationship, and when that failed terribly, I decided to just think about other stuff. But, like all things, her time away ended and she was back on her way to the northern part of the continent.

It was a Saturday when Anna came back. Actually, she got in late the night before, but I knew the girl needed her sleep, so a few texts was all I got. As I sat in my room earlier that day, finishing up some college essays and supplements for the schools I'd chosen to apply to, I got a call from Pete. Now understand that all of our best friendship communication was done either through text or in-person. There was nothing else, and there were sure as hell no long phone conversations where we poured our hearts out to each other. That just didn't happen. I think we may have actually spoken on the phone once or twice in our entire lives, so when I saw him calling instead of texting I picked up the phone right away.

"What's up? You okay? What the hell are you doing calling me?"

"I know," he said. "Planning, man, I'm planning. It's stressing me the hell out." He sounded frantic. As soon as I heard the tone in his voice I already knew what he was referring to, but I played dumb.

"Oh yeah? Planning what?"

"Our anniversary, what else?"

"That's sweet, man, I didn't even get you anything. Are you taking me out to a nice dinner? I'm not putting out, so get that out of your head."

"You think I want to sleep with you? You don't think I could do better than your skinny ass?" We both laughed hysterically. "But seriously, I'm trying to finalize some stuff and I need to know what the deal is with you two. I need to make this something special."

The hotel. In the haze of Peru I'd forgotten to even bring it up to Anna before she left. Maybe forgotten isn't the right way to say it, because I was aware that their anniversary was coming up but I still had no good way of asking Anna if she wanted to spend the night with me in a hotel room in the city.

"I still have to ask Anna. Do we even have enough tickets?"

"I bought enough for you and a girl a long time ago."

"Wait, what?" I asked. That was the first I was hearing about extra tickets and I was a little shocked. "How did you even know I'd have a girlfriend?"

"I didn't my friend, but I hoped. And apparently I have a sixth sense when it comes to your love life, so don't question it. But you've gotta man the hell up and just ask her already."

"Easy for you to say."

"Do you need me to throw another fry at your face?"

"Only if you want to get killed."

"Look, it's not as weird as you think. You're making it weird. Just ask her. I need to finalize reservations for next week."

"Alright, I'll ask her. You sound stressed as hell, by the way."

"You'd be stressed too, if you had to coordinate all this. It's a lot."

"I'm still pissed that you co-opted our Comic Con plans for your anniversary."

"Shit, man, we've already had this talk, you can't possibly be mad anymore. You're like a chick who can't let something go."

"That's a great way to resolve this situation, asshole, by insulting me."

"Maybe this is why we never speak on the phone. 'Cause you know if I was sitting in that room you wouldn't be so tough."

"Why don't you come by and find out."

Now this was not a real fight, just to be clear. This was best friend guy shit 101. Puffed chests, calling each other 'assholes', fake threats of kicking each other's asses. That was just what we did. It's what we all did. But it was all love. The one thing I was really pissed about was the Comic Con thing, though. Here's the story. Pete was low key a much bigger comic book geek than I was. Kid was hardcore, he just didn't wear it on his sleeve the way I did. Had you walked into my room at any point up to two years ago you would have seen X-men posters, boxes of Spider-Man comics, and enough collectible figurines to subsidize an undergraduate degree at Princeton. Pete was even worse, but he left no evidence of his crimes. He was clean, secretive, and didn't like anyone to know how into books he was.

We'd saved up our birthday money, and other funds we'd procured from selling off some of our lesser books online, so we could get some VIP tickets to Comic Con, and it was something I had truly looked forward to since the time we planned it out. Then came Lindsey. Now don't get me wrong, when I told you how great Lindsey was before I meant every word. I loved the girl, and she was as sweet as they came. She deserved the best anniversary that Pete could offer her. But don't get it twisted; she had no right to my Comic Con experience. Maybe that was immature of me to think, maybe I was being Petty Crocker, but that was our thing, and Pete sold me out. Fucker asked me to give up my ticket to his girlfriend, to which I told him to eat shit, as any self-respecting nerd would do when presented with such a ridiculous ultimatum.

Don't be a dick, he told me. *I'm not being a dick by not giving your girlfriend a ticket*, I told him, *go buy her one if you must, but what business does she have even coming with us?* No answer. There was an answer, actually, but it was too difficult for Pete to admit to himself or me. Kid was about as romantic as Jack the Ripper. No creativity, no original ideas. He was a good boyfriend, mind you, but when it came to rituals like anniversaries, Pete couldn't get anything good going. So what did his unoriginal self do? Right, he tried for some one-stop-shopping. Two birds, one stone. Our thing became their thing, and the dude tried to push me out like a hostile Comic Con takeover. Only my insistence that he was being a royal asshole got him to back off, but there was no convincing him to leave Lindsey out of it. He bought her a VIP ticket also, and apparently bought an extra ticket for the non-existent girl he thought I'd have at the time. Maybe he knew I'd talk to Annalise before I did.

Anyway, our best friend negotiations had yielded the situation we now found ourselves in: we were going to Comic Con as a foursome, with dinner and a hotel stay over to follow. And now I had to bring up the hotel issue to Annalise. Shit.

"Because I don't want to kick your ass in your own home. That would be embarrassing."

"Alright, alright," I said. "Enough of this. I'll talk to her, alright?"

"Today?"

"Sure," I said, getting more annoyed with each syllable on the other end of the phone. "Why not? I'm going to see her in a little bit anyway."

"Ok, let me know ASAP. Later."

"Later."

I felt like driving around a little. It was a pointless activity, but I enjoyed getting out of my neighborhood and seeing other places that I would have never walked to in a million years, so I asked Anna if she wanted to tag along. *Sure*, she said, *I could go for some aimless driving*. She worked Friday and Saturday nights at a burger place a town over, so we had to be back before three, which was when she got ready. It was a little past noon at that point, and I was set to pick her up in about a half hour.

When she jumped in the car I was nervous like it was the first time I'd ever talked to her before. It had only been two weeks since we'd seen each other but she took my breath away. Seeing her in person was a whole different experience than talking to her over text. She looked beautiful, but her face was stressed, and she strained to even smile at me. "Hey there," I said when she sat down.

"Hey."

"What's the matter?"

"Nothing," she said, clearly not wanting to talk. "Drama inside."

"Oh shit, I'm sorry. You just got back, what the hell could there be drama over already?"

"Don't worry, it's irrelevant, I'll live." She always said that. It was as if she was allergic to comfort, but I never stopped trying to make her feel better.

"I know you'll live, but if you need to get anything off your chest, I'm here to listen, you know?"

She leaned over and kissed me quickly, then sat back in her seat, staring forward through the glass. "Just drive away from here," she said. "That'll do the trick."

So I did. I'd learned not to pry too hard, but the truth of the matter was that her secrecy was starting to bother me more than a little bit. I felt like I'd told her things that no one else knew about me. I'd let her into some of the most secret places that I had inside of me, and told her things I didn't even tell Pete, but she didn't seem willing to do the same. Then I felt like a dick for feeling angry at her for not opening up to me as much as I wanted her to. After all, we all had our ways of coping with family drama, right? It wasn't about what I wanted, it was about what she needed. And apparently she needed to be really closed off and secretive. And I was the king of deflecting questions about my home life when I didn't want to talk about it. But I had this expectation that being in a relationship should have been different. If my girlfriend couldn't confide in me then maybe something was wrong with us. Wrong with me.

I decided to table that particular frustration because I had more important matters to discuss, and they were stressing me the hell out. I decided to drive a few towns away to the Land of the Rich People. After all, if I was going to drive around and look at cool stuff, why not hit the richest neighborhood I could find? It only took about ten minutes, but in that time Anna barely said a word to me. She didn't seem mad, she just seemed distant, like her mind was somewhere far gone from the passenger seat of my car. I tried to make small talk a few times—dumb stuff about school, asking what was wrong again—all of which she basically shut down with a simple one word answer, all the while staring out her side window.

"Look, I'm not trying to be annoying—"

"Well that's a good thing," she joked, cutting me off.

"But. . ."

"Oh, no."

"But you seem like you're a million miles away. If you didn't want to come out you didn't have to."

"You think I don't want to be here with you?" She loved to pivot like that in conversations. She'd flip your statement into a question that put you on the defensive and deflected from what you were trying to say to her. I wasn't biting today.

"I think that you wanted to get out of your house," I said blatantly. "And I was the way out of there. But you've barely said a word to me, so yes, you seem like you don't want to be here." It wasn't too forceful and I wasn't raising my voice or giving her any attitude, but it was a brutally honest statement meant to provoke some kind of response. Frankly, I would have taken anything other than apathetic silence, even if she wanted to scream and yell and jump out of the car while cursing my name. Well, not that, but you know what I mean. She pondered what I'd said for a minute.

"You're half right," she finally said to me.

"Which half?"

"I did just want to get out of my house. But I also wanted to be here with you. The two things just coincided. If I just wanted to leave I could have walked out the door and taken a long walk. I take a lot of those."

"You take a lot of long walks?" I asked.

"Yeah, all the time."

"Like how long is long?"

"I don't know," she answered. "I've never kept track, but I've walked around this neighborhood before."

"Wait, you've walked to where we are now from your house? That's got to be fifteen miles."

"Yeah," she said, sounding depressed. "Sometimes I just can't be home with them." It was weird, but the more she talked the more distant she sounded. "And anyway, how do you think I keep in good shape?" She tried to smile, but the joke fell flat. There was something about fake happiness meant to cover up real sadness that turned me right off —it was like those guys in gym who try to put on body spray or shitty cologne to cover up their BO.

"You know you can talk to me about this stuff, right? I feel like you keep everything bottled up. That's no good."

"I've heard that before," she said. "It's hard for me to open up, okay? It's not you, it's with everyone."

"I get that, but I'm not everyone." I could feel the conversation getting a little contentious, and I was getting a little angry. The point of hanging out wasn't to start a fight, so I decided to move on. "Anyway, let's change the subject."

"Great idea," she agreed, starting to sound a little annoyed herself.

I knew just how to change the subject. Let me rewind for a second. Anna's birthday was fast approaching, which of course meant that I had to get her a gift. It's not that I had to, per say, but I really wanted to. I was excited to actually be in a position to buy something for a girl, but I had no idea what to get her at first. I was out of my league when it came to stuff like that, so I did what anyone would do, I asked my more experienced friend for advice at lunch.

"How do you buy a gift for a girl?" It was a stupid question on its face, I knew, and Pete didn't miss his chance to point that out.

"That's a really stupid question."

"I'll rephrase. I've never bought a gift for a girl before and I don't know what to get or how much to spend. Like, is there such a thing as too much?"

"Definitely," Pete said. "But not because we guys can't afford it—I mean in most cases we can't—but it's more about the comfort level of the girl."

"Like how?" I asked.

"Well it depends. Some girls wanna be showered with expensive stuff. Others feel real uncomfortable with that, like they owe you something for it."

"Something?"

Pete raised his eyebrow at me. "You can't be that naive."

"Oh," I said, finally getting the point. "Well that's not how I'd mean it. I hope Anna would know that."

"I'm sure she would," Pete said, reassuring me. "But just to be safe, don't go nuts. Don't empty your bank account for something shiny. Get her something you know she'd like."

Something I knew she liked. That was a difficult one. Not knowing what to get her should have been my first red flag as to how little I knew about Anna's life, but in the fog of first love sometimes these things get missed. But after a few minutes of post-lunch-with-Pete contemplation there was one thing that popped into my head. I smiled ear to ear when I thought of it, and probably looked crazy as hell. If someone had been next to me at a traffic light and looked over at my crazy smile, I might have closely resembled a super villain who'd just had an epiphany on how to achieve world domination. But my smile was all pride.

The next day, after school, I took the car and drove to

the mall. Normally me and the mall had a worse relationship than me and school, but that day its existence was a
necessary evil. Luckily for me the store I needed was right
by the entrance to the parking lot, and thirty minutes after
my anxiety ridden walk through the side doors, I was
headed out of there with my gift-wrapped box in hand.
With Pete's voice in my head, I immediately worried that I
had spent too much money, but then again I had no idea
what too much was. I didn't really care, either. Back to us
in the car. . .

"What are you grinning at?" she asked me. "You look
like you did something wrong."

"No, I'm just happy."

"Oh, okay," she said, looking at me like I was being a
little weird, which in retrospect I probably was. "About
what?"

"Here." I handed her the gift, still in the bag from the
store, my dumb happy grin getting wider by the second.
She took it from me and started to unwrap it.

"What's this?"

"Happy birthday," I said. "I know I'm a little early but
I couldn't wait."

She opened the box and took it out. I did that weird
thing where I stare at a person's face while they open a gift,
and all I was waiting for was a smile.

I watched her pull the crucifix out of the box I'd asked
the guy at the store to gift wrap because, well, I sucked at
wrapping, and I wasn't about to let such a momentous
occasion as buying my girlfriend a first gift get screw up by
my inability to fold corners properly. She lifted it up slowly,
and my face lit up when I saw the smile on hers.

I'd thought forever on what to get her. I contemplated
the perfect gift for so long that I missed the obvious thing
that was right in front of me. Her faith. I told you how reli-

gious she was, right? Good Spanish girl and all that. She never talked about her faith unless you did something to offend it, which I probably did more than once. And I get the irony of the atheist giving his uber religious girlfriend a cross. But the truth of it was that even though I didn't believe myself, I loved how faithful Annalise was. In fact, it was one of my favorite things about her. The whole time we were together she never missed a Sunday service with her Mamita.

A word about Mamita is in order. Now just because she doesn't occupy these pages much that doesn't mean she isn't one of the most important people in the story you'll never actually meet. Mamita was Anna's grandma, who lived in a town over from ours. Not a week passed without Anna going over to her apartment to spend time with her at least a few days after school. I wasn't kidding when I said that I couldn't even talk to her on Sunday's until she got back from church. That was their thing—Sunday church. And for all the craziness in Anna's life, the one pure thing that seemed to ground her was her Mamita.

And that was what I thought of when I decided to get her the gold cross she was now dangling from her finger-tips, as the light from the sun reflected off it and onto her face. "I love this so much," she said, staring at it.

"Really?"

"Are you kidding me? This is the nicest thing anyone's ever gotten me. I love it."

"I hope that's not the best thing you've ever gotten before. You deserve way nicer than that, but it was all I could afford."

"It is," she said. "And I'm never going to take it off. Can you put it on me?"

I was so happy that she was happy. It's hard for me to describe to you just how her face looked when she really smiled. Not an obligation smile, not a polite grin, but the real thing. She didn't have too many unburdened smiles, but the once or twice I got to witness them were some of the purest moments of my own happiness. She lit up my car, and I unhooked the clasp and placed my cross around her neck.

"Thank you," she said, leaning into me. We kissed for what felt like forever, but it was probably only a few seconds. When our lips finally separated I felt my most vulnerable.

"You're welcome. And God, did I miss you so much."

"I missed you, too," she said. "But don't take the Lord's name in vain."

"Right, right, sorry."

"It's okay."

"I guess giving you a cross and then blaspheming is a bad mix, huh?"

"A little bit," she said smiling. "But I forgive you. Thanks for thinking of me."

"I kinda do that all the time. It's my full time job now."

"Oh yeah?"

"Yeah. Best job ever, by the way."

It wasn't my intention, but I'd interrupted our near fight with some birthday happiness, and then the anxiety came flooding back as I remembered that I still had to ask her about the city. I could feel my heart beating faster than hearts are supposed to beat. I always thought things like sweaty palms were some cliché in a romantic comedy, but I legit started to feel moisture building in my clenched hands. I took a deep breath to relax myself so she wouldn't think I was about to stroke out right there in the car, and she actually looked worried. "Are you alright?" she asked.

"Yeah, fine," I lied. But I knew I needed to spit it out before I had a full blown panic attack on this random person's street. "So, look, I wanted to ask you something before you left for Peru, but we were only together for a little while. . ."

"Okay." she said, waiting for me to spit it out.

"Pete, my best friend. Him and his girlfriend Lindsey—"

"Oh I love Lindsey," she said, cutting me off. "She's a really sweet girl."

"You know her?"

"Yeah. I mean, not well or anything. We're not friends, but she stood up for me once when these petty, little bitches in our grade were bullying me in gym freshman year. I always liked her after that."

"Oh, wow, I didn't know that happened. Small world." I was rambling, and a little shocked that we were playing six degrees of Pete. But I had to ask her already. "Anyway, he and Lindsey are celebrating their month-a-versary by going to Comic Con in the city."

"Wait, their what?"

"Don't ask. 11 months."

"Oh, I get it now. That's a new one."

"Yeah," I said. "Anyway, I know Comic Con sounds lame, but. . ."

"Lame? Are you nuts? I think that's like, the best anniversary ever. Or, month-a-versary gift, whatever. I've always wanted to go."

Now let's pause for a second in our conversation here for me to explain the emotions I was experiencing when she said that. I fell in love all over again. Only this time I pictured our wedding. Crazy. Stupid. Over the top. I know all this, but in that moment, I left my body. I was on some other plane of human existence, and while there I saw our wedding day. I saw Annalise waiting at the end of the isle dressed like Jean Grey during the Dark Phoenix saga—

minus the evil—and I was Cyclops, my whole narrow vision focused on the splendor of her mutant beauty. One day our son would be named Nathan, though the world will know him only as Cable.

Then I snapped back into reality.

"So, they have 4 tickets. It's a long story but this was a thing Pete and I were going to do, but somehow it became a Pete and Lindsey thing. Anyhow, do you wanna go? It's next Saturday."

"I'd love to," she said. "I'll have to tell work, but I'm sure it'll be fine."

"Great, it's settled. But also. . ."

"Oh, there's more?"

Here it went. Oh shit.

"Yeah. Afterwards they wanted to go to dinner. Kind of like a double date."

"Sounds good. I love eating in the city."

"And then. . ." I kept stopping myself. It was a sure fire way to sound as shady as possible.

"And then?"

"And then he and Lindsey are making hotel reservations at a place that's not too far from the convention center"

"That sounds really romantic," she said. That gave me the confidence I needed to get the last sentence out.

"I agree. So how would you feel about. . . I mean, it wouldn't be too weird if you and I. . . Do you think. . ."

"Logan Santiago, are you asking if I want to get a room with you?"

"You make it sound so dirty."

We both started laughing uncontrollably, and I actually felt much better that I had finally asked her, but then I realized that she hadn't actually answered me.

"I'd love to," she said. "I'd absolutely love to."

No words had yet been invented to explain how I was feeling, a weird mixture of relief, happiness, disbelief, and anticipation that I didn't know what to do with. It was like my body was electrified, and I didn't know what the hell to do with myself except to say, "That's awesome, we'll have a good time."

"I know we will," she said back, smiling.

At once I forgot about how she came out of her house, or how frustrated I'd been with her not communicating with me. I forgot it all because we were going to Comic Con next week, and I was just generally in a good place. We drove around and talked for a bit, and everything seemed to be normal.

The next few days at school were as normal as normal got, save for me getting to spend time with my. . .wait for it, girlfriend! We all got to hang out at school now, which was incredible in and of itself, and while it in no way made school enjoyable, it made it much more bearable. And I loved seeing Anna around my friends. Scratch that, my friend. She was funny as hell. Her impersonation of ghetto Spanish girl, specifically, was not to be missed. It was a hidden talent. Had there been a reality talent show for impersonating ghetto Spanish girls at the time, Anna would have been the Kelly Clarkson of that shit. If there were Oscars for it, she might have given Daniel Day Lewis a run for his top-hat wearing self. When she got into it, she embodied all those characteristics that I found abhorrent when they were real. Yeah, you're picturing it right, don't worry; hoop earrings (always gold, always big enough to jump small agility trained dogs through), tight little shorts (whether summer or not), curly hair that looks wet all day no matter what, and that particular brand of don't-mess-with-me-or-I'll-cut-you attitude radiating in every direction. Now even though she came from what you'd call the wrong side of the tracks, she was in no way ghetto, but she played it on TV. Nailed that shit perfectly, mostly when engaging in one of her favorite recreational sports— making fun of the girls at school who were really like that.

She didn't much like other girls. Like at all. We'd be hanging out in the cafeteria before school, just me, Anna, and Pete. Girls would walk by who I knew from class and I'd give a little lazy, under caffeinated morning wave and say *what's up*. About five to ten seconds later, usually with said girl still within ear shot, Annalise would look at her phone and give a low-key 'whore' declaration. *Wait, who*, I'd ask, *so-and-so? Nah, she's not at all*, I'd tell her. Then I'd get the eye. Actually what I really got was the eye-brow. Anna's right eyebrow had some crazy dexterity, 'cause she could raise that shit up like some angry, inverted half-moon, and when she did she made this intense eye contact that signi-fied that I'd messed right up. *Oh, really*, she'd say, *well how exactly would you know she's not a whore?* Cue Consuela.

I named Annalise's ratchet alter-ego Consuela after an inside joke Anna and I had about how it was such a stereo-typical Spanish name, yet no one actually knew anybody with that name. I mean, someone did, obviously, but we sure didn't, so it worked as a ratchet alter-ego moniker. Now, when Consuela made her entrance onto the stage, boy, you were in for a real treat. I'll break it down for you, it went something like this:

"Giiiirl, that bitch tried it, she tryyyd it, walkin' round in them little-ass shorts like it's the middle of July when she knows Christmas lights still hangin' on people houses. . .girl, get ya life!" Now, to picture what she looked and sounded like you have to imagine some physical gestures that go along with that accent and those dragged out sylla-bles. The hands. The hands were critical. When Anna went full Consuela, she'd wave her left hand in semi-circles next to her head, with her fingers touching; her head would jerk side to side for emphasis, usually about the 'get' part of her favorite expression, 'get your life.' We'd all break down laughing, mostly because she was spot on about whatever girl she was impersonating, but also because we all had dark senses of humor.

But back to my defense of 'whore' before. I knew I messed up the second I said it. Now Anna was mostly making me sweat just to do so, but I learned that messing up with her was something like eating undercooked pork at a friend's barbecue—it didn't hit you right away, but about 12 to 24 hours later you would realize that something was horribly wrong (was that scratch always on my car), you'd then retrace your steps (oh, shit, I called her a bitch when we had that argument), assess the damage (where the hell did my watch go, it was my grandfather's), and finally the acceptance that you'd have to just ride that shit out.

Like another time, same basic setting as before, when I made the novice, tactical error of calling another girl pretty. Actually, let me amend that. What I really did was fall into a trap. You know the one: she'd fake compliment some female passer-by, and then ask if I agreed or disagreed. Now, here's where my relationship inexperience showed itself. My thought was to agree with her point of view to show support, only Anna wasn't testing my support, she was testing my loyalty and sincerity. Big difference.

Oh you think that girl's pretty, she'd ask all innocent. Now I know what you're thinking even reading that—how could our boy be so stupid, right? Clear as day where that question is going. It wasn't stupidity my friends, it was inexperience. See, 17 year old Logan was not yet schooled in the ways of calculated females who can lay verbal traps in plain sight and still have you fall into them. And not those humane traps that kill you quickly, either, the ones that pierce you at the ankles, leaving you alive and flailing in pain until you die a slow death. So how did dumbass, never-had-a-real-girlfriend Me reply? You guessed it. *Yeah, she's very pretty*, I'd say. Sometimes I'd even add my own modifier just to naively show how much I agreed with Anna.

Let me explain what happened from there, if you haven't guessed already. You know that scary eyebrow raise your mom used as an intimidation tactic to get you good and scared when you did something wrong? Yeah, Annalise's eyebrow raise made your mom's seem like a warm massage delivered by cherubs high on weed. "Oh, she's VERY pretty, huh? That ho?" *Ummm, I guess*, I'd say, but the time for explanation had clearly ended because when a Spanish girl has her eyebrow arched over her rage-filled brown eyes like an upside-down U, best to internalize that the fight is over and you have lost. Word to the wise: don't ever sound like you're trying to defend the girl who your girl is calling a ho (or any other anger-induced pejorative her salty ass can come up with), just doesn't end well. You've been warned.

"OH, so she's a really nice person AND she's very pretty? I see. Say no more. Say nooo more." At that point I should've followed that advice and literally said no more, but the stubborn part of me just couldn't let stuff like that go, even with Anna. I reiterated my disagreement with Anna's assessment of the girl, and I got a second eyebrow-lashing. I could defend myself against these kind of feminine assaults simply by looking away—like avoiding looking directly at the sun or not sitting too close to the TV when you were a kid; but Anna was a guerilla—trained in all manner of non-conventional warfare, and if you put up a solid defense against one attack, that's exactly when the secondary and tertiary attacks would come, and there were only so many defenses you could put up. *Oh, okay*, she said, *so you're saying she's prettier than me? No no*, I'd protest in my full reactionary glory, *that's not what I meant.* Now, Anna knew damn well I didn't mean that, and that I didn't even say that, but once she had me on the defense she had already won our little game.

Sometimes she got fake mad. She'd text me "ouch" when I'd say things not even meant to make her feel some type of way. Like the time I told her she wasn't sweet. Well, actually, she texted me and told me that she was the sweetest, to which I called swift and accurate bullshit. *You're not sweet*, I told her. Got my requisite "ouch". Had to explain myself. *No no*, I told her, *that's a good thing, trust me. How is not being sweet a good thing*, she asked. It was a valid question, but I had an answer. I always had an answer. *Here's why*, I told her, *you're thinking 'sweet' is like 'nice' - like they're synonyms. They're not, trust me. When you say that about a girl you're describing her disposition, not her actions*, I tried to explain. *The sweet girls were those giggly, kinda dumb, overly innocent girls who were waiting around to have the sweet victimized right out of them. You aren't sweet*, I told her. *If you started smiling all the time and thinking the best of people I'd shake the hell out of you and demand a drug test.* Got my smiley face emoji back, she understood. *No, no*, she wrote, *that's not me. Thank god*, I told her, and then I got shit for using the lord's name in vain. I mentioned that she was Peruvian right? Catholic as they come? Thought so. Just checking.

"Pete," she said in her normal voice as we all sat around waiting for the dregs of first period to come. "Solid idea on the anniversary. I applaud you, Sir."

"Thanks, Anna, tell your boy. He's still salty about the whole thing."

"No, I'm all good, man," I said. "All makes sense. The force has balance."

"Look at Mr. Chill over here," Pete joked. "You must be having a positive effect on him; he's usually up for a fight when it comes to this topic."

"I don't know what could have ever changed his mind." Anna was being coy. She knew exactly what had changed my mind – the promise of being there with her. I was so psyched about it that it almost superseded the excitement I had for the event itself. I felt like I was maturing as a person when I wanted the girl over the signed books and panels. I was growing up.

"Well, whatever it was, I'm sure it's due to you. And we're happy to have you there with us."

"Are you kidding? I'm the happy one, and I don't get to say that often. Thanks again for the invite."

"You're welcome."

First period came. Then second, and before I knew it, ninth. The days went faster when I was with her; their passing hours seeming less like a prison sentence and more like what I needed to do in order to spend time with her afterwards. As we headed into the late winter I felt generally lighter. Mom was having some good days, the horizon line of school was foreseeable, and I was about to go to Comic Con with my girl.

That's right, let me say it again, *with my girl*.

NINE

Where two nerds escort their girlfriends to nerd Heaven.

We stood in line for thirty minutes before getting inside what was, at that point in my life, a nerd's Mecca. Literally. It was the holy land, the sacred space where geekdom hosted its annual pilgrimage. The gaming and comic fans were in full force, dress-up optional, and we tried to hit every possible stand, signing, and panel.

The whole day was greater than great. That doesn't even do it justice. Whatever combination of letters or words expressed the heights of what a person can feel, that's how I felt being in the city with everyone. Pete and I were among our people, me especially, but being in that place with Anna was an unlocked bonus stage of an experience. I knew that comics weren't her thing, but if she wasn't having as good a time as me I never knew it. She was the ultimate supportive girlfriend, and she seemed to really be taking in the experience. If you've never been, there's a LOT of walking around at Comic Com, like, a lot a lot. If you measured it you probably had half a marathon's worth of nerd travels. So after an hour or so we stopped to map out our next moves and take a few deep breaths.

"I'll be right back," Anna said to me suddenly.

"Okay, no problem."

She went off on her own, disappearing quickly into the crowd, and I really had no idea where she was running off to. I assumed she had to go to the bathroom or something, but Lindsey didn't do that weird female thing where she offered to go with her, so who knew? In the meantime Pete and I checked out a counter that was selling classic X-Men figurines so expensive that we each would have had to sell a kidney on the black market to even afford one of them.

"Holy shit."

"I know," I said. "These prices are nuts."

"That's not even close to the right word for how much that Magneto one costs. Who the hell can spend that much on a little statue?"

"Rich people."

"Who?" he asked. "Everyone here is like our age?"

"Okay, then rich kids I guess."

"These aren't collectibles, they're investments."

"Yeah, I'm not into investing in statues. Even if I had the money I wouldn't spend it on these."

"Then what?"

"What do you mean?"

"Like, if you had the money, what would you spend it on?"

That was a great question, but it was also an easy one. "Simple," I told him. "That copy of Wolverine number 1 signed by Frank Miller and Chris Claremont that I saw back when we first walked in."

"Damn, that's a good choice."

"Thank you. But this is all hypothetical. I pooled all of my funds for dinner and the hotel."

"Same. I'm just here for the experience. And I have to say, I'm having a good time."

"Me, too," I said. "But what about the girls? Do you think they're just humoring us?"

"Oh, totally. But isn't that what boyfriends and girl-friends are supposed to do for one another?"

"You'd know better than me, man. I've only had one."

We stood around for a little while just sipping our water bottles and looking at more stuff we could never afford, and before too long Annalise appeared behind us and yelled "Boo", and tapped me on the shoulder.

"Shit, you scared me," I said, laughing. "Where'd you run off to?"

"Bathroom. Lines were crazy but it moved super-fast. You boys in the market for statues?"

"Only when we take our company public," Pete joked. "Before that I don't think we could scratch together enough money for even the head of one."

"I think you could do the head. You guys don't give yourselves enough credit."

"You're right," Pete joked, looking at me. "You wanna go in on a Professor X head?"

"Only if you wanna go straight home after this with no food."

"Got it. Screw Professor X. Let's move on."

The next few hours went by like they were minutes. Nerds everywhere, being cool by not being cool at all. It was a blast, and after we did even more walking and window shopping it was time to bounce and head to dinner. Pete had decided to do his best impersonation of a grown up and actually made reservations at some restaurant he found on Yelp. Some Italian joint that sounded nothing short of delicious, and to be honest we could have grabbed a dirty water dog on the street and I would have been happy. I was on cloud nine. But, alas, we wouldn't be dining on disgusting hot dogs; we were going out for a legit meal in the city.

The problem with being so far in my own head was that I didn't think of the food issue. Excuse me, issues. It never even occurred to me that Annalise might not have something to eat at wherever we went. I'd outsourced the whole thing to Pete, probably because I secretly wanted to forget all of the bizarre food related issues Anna had, but one thing I knew for sure was that steak probably wasn't on the menu.

When we got to the place my first thought was how underdressed we were. Thank God we weren't in Legend of Zelda costumes or something crazy, it would have been dirty water dogs all night, because no respectable place would have dared seat us looking like that. As it was, the place wasn't overly fancy, but we were easily the youngest and most casually dressed people in the place. I noticed, but I didn't really care. I always thought that in a situation like that, everyone in the place would turn around and look at us in our Jeans and judge us, or that the waiter would speak in a snobby accent and treat us like crap. See, movies again. They ruin you. In reality no one cared about us because they were busy eating their own dinners.

We felt like real adults. It was kind of weird. Pete and I had money to pay, we pulled out the girls chairs, the waiter handed us menus. Adults. Dinner went way more smoothly than I thought. I stared at Anna like a weirdo because I was waiting for her to have some serious menu struggles. I was terrified that our waiter, ill-informed in the ways of Annalise, would tell us about some special that was a soup, followed by her near gagging at even the mention of her culinary kryptonite. But it never happened. Apparently pasta was ok. She liked pasta, and our dinner went off without a hitch. It was great to eat with everyone after such a great day. Afterwards Pete and I split up the bill and paid, and we went outside to get cabs to the hotel.

We decided to take separate cabs rather than squeeze into one. The hotel was a little farther from the restaurant than any of us wanted to walk. Our legs were shot from our nerd walking, and we were willing to pay for a little pampering. Pete and Lindsey got in theirs first, and I hailed a second one right behind them. Once we were inside I gave the guy the address to the hotel and we sat in some pretty serious city traffic to get there. "Dinner was good," she said to me.

"Sorry they didn't have steak. Pete chose the place."

"I eat other things besides steak, silly. It's okay, but thanks for worrying."

"How was the pasta?"

"Really good, actually. I'm going to need you to make that for me one day."

"I'm pretty sure I can do that."

"Before we get to the place I wanted to give you something."

"What?" I asked.

Anna reached into her giant bag. She told me to close my eyes, which I did because she told me to, but I wasn't sure what the hell was actually happening. "Are they closed?"

"Uh-huh."

"Here." I heard the crinkling of paper, followed by on object in my hand. I knew right away what it was, and I was amazed, but until I opened my eyes it wasn't real.

"Holy shitballs," I yelled as I looked down. Sitting in my hands was a signed, graded copy of Wolverine 1, signed by Frank Miller and Chris Claremont. "Is this real?"

"If it's not I really overpaid for it."

"Oh my God, how did you know?"

"Well I saw you staring at it for like three minutes and I kind of figured it was special to you. You didn't do that with any other books."

"Wolverine is my favorite. All time."

"How come? Why Wolverine?"

"Do you know the story?" Annalise nodded. "He was this guy who got kidnapped and went through a terrible trauma. They tried to make him into this weapon—a perfect killing machine—but it was torture. He went through hell. But after he went through all of that he came out stronger on the other side. They couldn't kill him. And not only that, he became, like, the strongest mutant there was."

"That's a pretty cool story."

"Yeah," I said. "But seriously, how?"

"My family in Peru gave me some money for my birthday. I told you they have money, right? They took care of me."

"Yeah, but I'm sure you need the money for other stuff. You didn't have to spend so much on me."

"I know I didn't," she said, putting her hand over mine, which was still clutching the book like my life depended on it. "I wanted to. You looked so happy." She leaned in and kissed me, and I was like a kid on Christmas morning.

"You're the best, do you know that?"

"I know," she joked.

Even with the crazy traffic our two cabs got to the hotel around the same time. The place was beautiful, and once we went inside we went to our neutral corners, with a promise to meet up for breakfast the next morning. Pete wanted to high-five me, but that shit seemed a little too teen boy even for me. So Anna and I checked in first and brought up the little overnight bags we had packed. It still seemed shady to me to bring a girl to a hotel and not pretend that mattered, but Anna didn't seem to think so.

We spent the first hour or so in continued frivolity, the exact same way we had ended dinner. A combination of small talk and crappy TV shows that I couldn't stand but Anna couldn't seem to get enough of. She loved those panel shows, the ones where minimally talented and famous women sit around a table and yelled opinions at one another. For someone so intelligent, she had an almost insatiable appetite for bad television. I didn't care. I was just happy to be along for the ride, and I'd lay with her as she giggled and laughed at the people on the screen, happy to be that close to her at all.

"These shows are ridiculous," I said.

"You're ridiculous."

"What do you even get out of this, anyway?"

"They're funny," she said. "They make me laugh."

"But you're not laughing."

"Inside I am. I'm a barrel of laughs on the inside."

When the TV shows were over she seemed to open up for the first time in a while. It was one of the few times I remember her being open with me without me asking too much. I did ask her how she liked to sleep.

"Total darkness," she told me. "If there's any light on, I can't sleep."

"Yeah, me too." That was as much of a lie as I ever told her. I was terrified of sleeping in the dark, even at seventeen. I would have slept with a spotlight shining in my face like an interrogation suspect in one of those crime shows, but I was willing to trade a little white lie so she could sleep in comfort.

"And I love my blanket. I wrap myself up like a burrito. Don't make one of your Spanish girl jokes!"

"I promise. Well, I mostly promise."

"Mostly promise?"

"98% promise," I joked. "But if you set up a pun so perfectly for me, how can you blame me? Come on now."

After about an hour I noticed a change in Anna. I couldn't tell you exactly what it was, but something obvious enough for me to tell that things had shifted in her mood. She was quiet at first, and when I tried to speak to her she didn't make much eye contact, and only gave me one word answers. At first I thought I'd done something wrong but then I realized that I hadn't done anything at all, I was just lying there. We were inches away from each other, watching TV in bed, but she felt a million miles away, and I started to worry.

I remembered learning about rationing in social studies; how during the World Wars some things were so scarce that people had to use limited quantities, or be issued certain amounts by the government. Annalise did the same thing, only instead of food or clothing she rationed herself. She never gave you much, a little at a time, and sometimes nothing at all, that was all that I was ever allowed. But each time felt special. Each time she told me a story about when she was little, or let me know a preference she had in foods, or told me anything, really.

I learned never to demand anything because forcing the issue just didn't seem to work. Actually it had the opposite effect, like struggling in quicksand. Instead I let her come to me, I let her know that she could trust me with the depths of her secrets and that I would protect her dreams with my very life. I let her know this with every letter, with every kiss, with every declaration of my feelings, until that exact moment when she evaluated me to be trustworthy.

I leaned into her slightly, and put my hand on her shoulder to get the attention my voice wasn't quite getting, and when I touched her she looked at me as though I'd woken her from a dream. Like I said, I wasn't going to force anything, I was only going to ask.

"The *Bleh*?"

She nodded without any hesitation, and I knew that saving her the energy of saying the word would help make her honest, but what I didn't expect was how that one little question let her open up in ways that she never did before or after that night. It was there that she opened her world to me, and allowed me glimpses, however small, behind that reinforced lead door that guarded her soul. I gave Anna the softest eyes I could I return. We understood each other, in tragedy, in love.

There, lying in bed, she told me about the Thoughts, the bad ones. She said they came late at night, when her friends and family weren't around, and they whispered to her how worthless she was, over and over, until she had no other desire than to harm herself. *They started when I was thirteen*, she said, *and they've always been there since, even at times when I seem happy and light-hearted. What caused them*, I asked. She didn't know, but they came to her specifically when she fought with her mom, which was often, and usually involved hateful screaming matches, with unkind words yelled in the loudest Spanish. In those exchanges, declarations of dislike, disdain, and wishes for Annalise to never have been born rang out through the house like a cacophony. And after the screams, copious tears, running fast and hard down faces contorted in anger, and after the tears, the Thoughts.

"You can't listen to them," I told her. "You're the most amazing person I've ever met. That stuff isn't real, it's just your mind playing tricks on you."

"I know, but it's hard to remember that when you're feeling it." She told me how convincing they were. *Maybe you were a worthless piece of shit, Anna, and maybe life would have been easier on your family without you; maybe it still could be.* She said they lasted hours, days sometimes, and weeks on occasion. They took up space in her mind and spoke in her mom's voice. Nothing made the Thoughts go away fully: no distraction, no social media scrolling, no amount of TV. Only one thing worked, she said, a flesh sacrifice to the Bleh gods, so Annalise gave them what they demanded, if only to get a few moment's peace.

The first time she did it she used a small knife from her kitchen drawer. "It didn't hurt nearly as much as I thought it would," she told me. "It didn't hurt at all. It felt good, actually. I felt alive." In so many words she told me that cutting herself was liberating, like a deep exhale. "When I looked down the first time there was a small pool of blood on the floor, right by my big toe." *Was that my blood*, she wondered. *But it couldn't be blood*, she convinced herself, *because when you bleed you have to feel pain; have to scream out in distress and demand to be bandaged and stitched. But that wasn't the case at all. There was no pain at all*, she told me. In fact, the blood had taken the pain all away; it fell out of her body and covered her bathroom floor, and then came the silence. *No more hateful words in Mom's voice*, she told me, *no more telling me I was worthless. Just relief.*

"The relief doesn't last," she said, the tears starting to roll off of her face and bathe the hotel comforter beneath us. "You have to keep doing it, and before you know it you're doing it so much that. . ."

"That what?" I asked.

"That you know how crazy you are. But you can't do anything to stop it." After a time the self-loathing returned, only this time the voice telling Anna that she was a useless, ugly piece of shit, wasn't her mother's, it was her own. And then the shame. The mark that spit her painless blood onto the floor of her bathroom now reminded her of her own weakness, and she hated the way she looked when she looked in that long mirror that hung on the back of her door.

When she was done telling me all of that I went to put my arm around her out of instinct, but she recoiled. *I hate that*, she told me, *please don't try to comfort me*. I did as I was told, but all that my arm wanted to do was reach around and clutch her back, and all my mouth wanted to do was form the perfect series of words, spoken just right, so that maybe I could make everything better again. But no such thing happened, because she asked me not to comfort her, and respecting her boundaries meant more to me than acting the role of what I thought a good boyfriend should be.

She told me what it was like to be unwanted by both a father who had abandoned her when she was nothing but a protrusion in her mom's belly, and by a mother who constantly told Anna that she was worthless. Instead of telling her what I couldn't promise was the truth, I told her what was inside my heart. I let her know that anyone who didn't want her was a fool, and even if there were such people in the world—even if she called them Mom—that she wasn't just wanted, but needed by me. I'm lost without you, I told her, as I wiped a tear from her cheek, and even when the world around her was blind, I saw. I saw her beauty; I saw her kindness; I felt the warmth of her heart infuse energy into my tired body, and I told her that I wanted her more than I could ever tell her, no matter how much I wrote to her.

She smiled of course, and whispered that she loved me. It echoed in a soft, bittersweet tone that made kissing her a mandatory act. And as I did, the feeling of her lips induced my heart to beat with that rapidity that only happened when I kissed her. I told her that as long as I was alive, she'd never be unwanted, and even though I couldn't ease the pain of her mom's cruelty, I could at least offer her a counter narrative. And that narrative was as follows: I loved her like I didn't know was possible, and every glance at her face left me breathless and insecure, because who the hell was I to deserve her? How on Earth could there be someone who made me so happy and in love? I told her that while I didn't know the answers to these questions, I would never stop asking, because she was my own personal goddess in human form, and her being unwanted was unfathomable.

She kissed me again, shifting her weight on me with a bump of her hip, forcing me to my back and throwing her legs over me. I was surprised at first, mostly at her agility and grace, let alone the fact that I was underneath her. She kissed me so intensely that I didn't know what to do with myself, her hair ticking the skin of my face. It was as if everything she never was able to tell me with words were expressed through the touch of her lips. In them I felt her passion, her love for me, and the connection we'd made with one another.

What happened next is for Anna and I, and that's where I'll keep it, forever.

<><><>

The next morning I woke up way before Anna. I'd slept like the dead, but I'd also woken up pretty early. I couldn't remember a better night's sleep, but it was also kind of a weird feeling to be rested. We all spent so much of our time under slept, overwhelmed, and generally in a slow and steady process of burnout that to just sleep well with no interruption or stress had me feeling weird. A good weird, but weird nonetheless. I was never able to stay in bed once I was awake, so I left Anna to her dreamland and washed up. After that I stood by the window of our room that overlooked the parking lot and reflected on the previous night. It was one I knew I'd remember forever, and technically the whole experience wasn't quite over yet. After a few minutes of staring at the people coming and going in the lot I turned and gazed at Anna. She looked angelic; peaceful.

After a minute she stretched her arms over her head as she slept, and that's when I saw them—two flowers tattooed on her right inner forearm. She'd told me about them before when we first met but like so many things with her, it took a while for me to truly see them. Two flowers, each representing a different time she overcame the struggles in her life. Her ink, which she was technically still too young to get legally, represented an anniversary of sorts, the day she'd recovered from her eating disorder and cutting issues. They were simple designs, but as I looked at them, scarred onto her arm, I realized that we all bear scars of the past. She was just creative enough to commemorate them.

"Morning," I said, when I saw her start to open her eyes.

"Uhhh," she groaned, stretching her arms up. "What time is it?"

"Six-Thirty. Pete and Lindsey are up, sort of. They're getting up, anyways. I just spoke to him. They wanna get breakfast after we check out."

"How dare you wake me up at such an obscene hour," she joked. Well, it wasn't really a joke; this was probably the earliest she'd been up in a while outside of school.

"Sorry," I said. "Do you forgive me?"

"Okay, fine." She smiled at me and I sat down on the side of the bed next to her. In the creeping of light from the window hitting her face, she looked magical to me. Her black hair fell to one side of her shoulders, and the vulnerability of waking up made her smile lighter than it normally was. I took a mental picture of her then. It's still my favorite one of her.

"How did you sleep?"

"Great," she said. "Like a girl wrapped in a burrito in total darkness, sleeping next to the guy she loves. How could I go wrong?"

Her words hit me in a way that made me fall in love with her all over again, as words can sometimes do if they're spoken by the right person. For once I decided not to speak with my words, and to instead just lean over and kiss her as deeply as I could, in a way that let her know what she let me know last night; that I loved her more than the waking world, and that when I was with her nothing else existed.

"Now I'm hungry. Where are we going?"

"The diner," I told her. "Where else?"

"Right," she said. "We have to go back don't we?"

"Back where?"

"Home. I guess we always have to go back home."

"They say that it's where the heart is, you know?"

"Who are they?" She asked.

"You know, they."

"Who?"

"I don't know," I said, frustrated at the fact that she was actually demanding a source for my crappy attempt at inspirational words. "I heard it somewhere. They said it."

"*The Council of They* again."

"Who?"

"That's what I call them. My sister does that all the time. She's always giving me the 'they says' to prove a point, but she never knows who *they* are. Sometimes it's *them* instead, like *according to Them*, or whatever. Why do we say that?"

"I don't know. You're right. I actually don't know who they are, but I know someone once said that home is where the heart is. I'll look it up later and get back to you."

"Whoever said that was full of it, or maybe they just came from a happy house. I hear those exist somewhere."

"Me too," I said, pretending that she was joking. "Maybe no one comes from a happy home at first, maybe it's something that you have to make for yourself one day."

"Maybe," she agreed. "But remember that every messed up Mom and Dad said that. They made their own homes, and look how it turned out."

"I think we're generalizing a little bit," I said, but I took her point. I wanted to change the subject because I knew she could go down this bitterness rabbit hole where interesting conversation could easily devolve into just being jaded. But I felt the need to be the light to her dark, so I kept it going for a few more exchanges. "Not everybody comes from a messed up home."

"Where did you grow up?" she asked. "Where I'm from happy homes are like Big Foot—everyone's got a story of their existence yet no one's actually seen or been inside one. I guess they exist, who knows. But from my experience, you have to go somewhere else to find them."

"Yeah," I said. "Maybe." Just then Pete texted again and the sound startled me a little. He wanted to check out and get some food. "Can you be ready in twenty?"

"Fifteen. Let me go shower."

She jumped out of bed and went into the bathroom. I had already gotten ready, so I sat on the bed doing what I did best back then, overthink things. But her words stuck with me, always, and I started reflecting on what she said to me as I heard the muffled sounds of water hitting the shower floor. Here's one thing I learned as a kid, and something I still believe as a man looking back: the people who screw us up owe a debt that can never be repaid. In fact, in a final poetic swell of victimization, the debt becomes ours. We have a chance to pay it back, or to leave it to our own children, as it was left to us. We have a choice, in other words, to make our damage into strength, or to make it into a family legacy. I didn't know which side of that I'd end up on at the time, but it was clear which side Anna was already falling onto. She didn't want to be bitter, and she sure as hell didn't want to be as messed up as she was, but it had been passed to her like a genetic trait, like her hair or eye color, and it would have been easier for her to change one of those things than it would have been for her to just be normal.

Maybe there was still hope for her, if hope wasn't for suckers.

Interlude

MY OPEN LETTER TO ANNALISE'S DAD, WHEREVER HIS PUNK ASS MIGHT BE.

Sir Whatever-the-Hell-Your-Name-Is,

There are other salutations I could have used, all equally fitting of your obvious propensity for sucking at being a human being: dear Nameless Faceless Sperm Donor; dear Poor Excuse For a Man; dear. . .oh, you get the idea. Actually you probably don't, 'cause if you got the idea you'd be here right now, in front of me, and I'd be calling your dumb ass by your actual name. I'd be calling you Sir for real, as in "Sir, I'm here to ask Anna to prom." But you and I don't get to have those moments. I don't get to call you Sir for real. We don't get to lock eyes and fight back our man-tears when you walk her down the aisle as I wait. Nah, that shit just isn't in the cards for us.

Instead you get my open letter. I wanna be a writer, did you know that? One day you'll walk into a bookstore and you'll pass a table where my latest and greatest is sitting in a big old pile. You'll pick it up and read the back, see the praise from the New York Times, maybe see my picture in the bottom right corner. Hell, you might even buy it and give it a read, who knows, but you'll never know who I am to you. That's the guy who loved your daughter more than anything in the world. Anna, your baby daughter who isn't a baby anymore. I've been going on and on about you and me, haven't I? But you and I don't really matter. You're nothing to me and you don't know I exist, and that's just fine. But as far as Anna goes, you've got no excuses there, Sir.

Oh you don't even know her name, do you? It's Annalise. Her mom named her that 'cause you weren't there to do so. She's seventeen years old now. How old are you? Old enough to regret? Old enough to look back on your decisions in life and be ashamed? Ah, screw it, who cares. Why should I spend even a minute of my time wondering about your internal processes? I shouldn't, but I bet Anna has. I bet deep down inside of her, in that hidden place that makes us who we are, she has only questions where she should have statements. Too many interrogatives and not nearly enough declaratives, know what I mean? Probably too stupid to even follow me, so let me break it down. When she thinks of herself she doesn't hear a voice telling her how great she is, she hears a voice asking questions like "why didn't he want me" and "wasn't I good enough?" You did that, Sir. And I don't care if you cure all the Cancers in the known world one day, you'll always be a failure, 'cause you missed out on knowing the greatest girl ever.

But don't you worry, she's no victim. She inspires me. She makes me understand that things are possible when I don't believe. She's my savior and sometimes, when she lets me be, I'm hers too. She's got a character like parents only dream of cultivating; morals beyond reproach; warmth of heart, kindness; and the girl doesn't know what a lie is. Who else do you know like that?

So, in conclusion, you, Sir, are a gargantuan pile of steaming dog shit, as both a father and a human being in general, but this is ancillary. I could take shots at you all day, but forget all that and remember only this: whoever you are and wherever you are, if you live to be 150 and have 10 other children, you'll never be anything but a failure to me, because you're the one thing that I can never give to the girl who deserves the world. And for that I'll never stop hating you, even if she did.

Sincerely, Logan Rosario Santiago

TEN

Where I tell you about our fights, both real and fake, and where Petty Crocker makes his triumphant return to the narrative.

Remember my disclaimer when you started this thing a while back? The one where I told you this wasn't your conventional love story, and that not everything ends picture perfect? I just wanted to remind you of that before we moved on.

After Comic Con, the next few months went along like normal for everyone. All of us were happy to be ending that crazy social experiment called public school, but scared for what came next at the same time. Like any complex emotional experience, we all handled it in our own ways. Pete went full Pete and didn't bring any of it up. That didn't mean he wasn't feeling the same things we all were, but he wasn't expressive like that. Anna didn't discuss the future, like ever, almost as if it was an abstract concept to her that was a waste of time to get into. And me? I was surrounded by people I felt like I couldn't quite talk to about certain things, so I just did what I always did, I wrote it down.

As far as Anna and I went, things were good for a while after our trip to the city that fateful night. It wasn't until a little bit after that I started to see the wheels coming off of our relationship. I could look back, biased as hell, and tell you it was all her, and that I was just a nice guy doing my best, but that would be some bullshit that would insult what really happened, as well as your intelligence. So understand I'm telling my account of things; my interpretation; my story. If you wanna know hers, go ask her, wherever she might be, I still have her number if you need it.

So nothing happened, per say. The beginning of the end was less Big Bang than it was the culmination of a lot of little things. But if I'm being honest, it was my frustration that started to expose the cracks. Like I said, she could be super secretive, and at first I had blinders on because I was so happy to even be with her that I was willing to overlook some things that bothered me. But over time I came to realize that she wasn't really hiding from me: she was hiding from a past that I had little knowledge of, and only deduced through the fractions of stories she chose to share. There were never moments like in the movies with us, never a long conversation where she just told stories about her past and I sat with a comforting arm around her. I got only broad strokes.

"You never tell me about your Mom," I told her once. "You know all about mine. Why don't you ever talk about her?"

"Well, what do you wanna know?"

That question killed me. It was the international code for *I'm gonna make you work to find shit out.* But I was game to play along, I had questions ready. "Let's start basic. What's her name?"

"Monica."

"Monica, great!" I said, realizing how dumb it sounded.

"Is it?"

"No, not her name, I meant great that. . .nevermind. Your mom's name is Monica, got it."

"What else?" she asked.

"What does she do for a living?"

"She's too screwed up to work." That sounded familiar. My mom had been on psychological disability since I was kid, only this sounded different. "Stereotypical as it sounds, she used to work doing housecleaning in some of the richer neighborhoods until she hurt herself."

"So what happened? She doesn't do that anymore?"

"One day when she was cleaning a window she leaned on it and sliced her hand on the pane of glass as it broke. She got fired for breaking a window and the lady took the money out of the small amount she paid my mom. Then we got stiffed with the emergency room bill later on. We didn't have insurance, so the visit and stiches cost us a few hundred dollars that took forever to pay off."

"Shit, I'm sorry."

"It was a few years ago. She hasn't worked since, so my older sister and I contribute to pay the rent. That's why I work. I don't really need the money for myself." She wasn't kidding about that. She was about the most low mainte-nance girl imaginable, like I said before. Not only did she not have any expensive or fancy things, she didn't want them. I guess being raised so poor taught her the value of money that most of us honestly didn't have until much later in life."So is she depressed like my Mom is? What do you mean by messed up?"

"Why do we have to talk about this?" she asked. To me it seemed obvious; I wanted to get to know who she was and where she came from, but it was always like pulling teeth to find anything out.

"We don't," I told her. "Never mind, it's fine."

Trying to decode her family life or her past was like a

jigsaw puzzle with only five center pieces—disjointed and incomplete—but it was all she ever gave me, and if I ever asked for more the subject got changed quickly. Sometimes I'd text her and ask what she was doing when I was bored at home, and instead of telling me she'd just want to know why I even asked.

"Why does that matter?" she'd say.

"Just asking." I'd tell her.

"Are you, like, keeping tabs on me?"

"No, I'm literally just making conversation. You could say you were anywhere and it's fine, I'm just asking."

Then I'd get, "I'll text you later. I'm out with some friends."

It was through conversations and fights like I just described, that I started to see the differences between the homes Anna and I came from. It was true that from the outside we seemed similar. Two Spanish kids (albeit one of them fake) from messed up homes, with mentally ill moms, and dads who'd fled the coop a while back. But the more I found out about her home life, the more I saw the differences. Her Mom seemed to have broken her, and mine was the complete opposite. I knew she felt guilty that I had to take care of her; that she felt like a burden because she knew I couldn't help but get caught up in her depression and anxiety.

When I say Anna had been broken I know it made her sound as if she was fragile and weak, so maybe it would be better to say that parts of her had been broken so young that she never learned the difference between being fucked up and being normal, like she had a type of emotional blindness that made her unaware that the way she was wasn't healthy. Imagine your toaster had a busted handle, or didn't actually toast your bread when you pressed the lever down. Now imagine being so unaware of that fact that every time friends or family came over, you offered them a nice crispy piece of toast with that gourmet black-berry jam you just got at Whole Foods. Now, if that man in my silly hypothetical really existed, I'd like to think one of his family members or friends would pull him aside and tell him stop offering everybody a piece of toast. But fixing emotional damage isn't as simple as getting your crazy, delusional ass to the store to get a new toaster. That kind of broken took a special someone to even recognize its existence.

I knew the difference because even though my home life had never been perfect, things were pretty good before Mom had her breakdown. I'd seen the world before and after the crash, so I had a basis of comparison, a perspective that Anna severely lacked, and because of that it made telling her anything really difficult. She didn't want to hear from me on issues with her family, not even to help. Actually, she *especially* didn't want me to try to help.

She'd listen for hours as I vented about whatever was bothering me, and she was, to date, one of the best listeners I've ever met. And if you think that's a minor thing then you haven't met that many people in your life, because to be truly heard is a rare thing indeed. After I spilled my guts to her it was like therapy, and she'd chase away my anxiety like carefully dosed Xanax, minus the Xanax. She'd look at me with such loving, intense focus that she made me believe my words were the most impor-tant ever uttered my Man. This never wavered in Anna— she was never too tired or too busy to listen—*I'll always listen*, she'd say, but when it came to confrontation, we interacted in a different way entirely.

The first time 'it' happened (our little fights became 'it' when we worked them out after the drama had subsided, as in *let's talk about it*) I'd just had enough of her being secretive. See, she never even agreed with my classification.

"Why are you being so weird and secretive?" I'd ask over a text or in a conversation, to which I'd get back something like the following.

"I'm not being secretive. Just 'cause I don't tell you every little thing doesn't mean I'm hiding it from you."

"Actually, that's literally the definition of secrecy, Anna. Why are you so worried about why I wanna know what happened that day you were (*fill in the blank here, there are a number of words that would have completed this type of sentence back then: crying, complaining, sad, weird, distant. . . all those work*)?"

"I'm done," she'd write back.

"With what?"

"With this," she'd say. Now what exactly *this* was, was itself a matter of debate—being occasionally insecure I'd think she meant the entire relationship, but more often than not what she meant was *let's change the subject, please*.

What always messed me up about our fights was not only the fact that they were happening at all, but how they always seemed to creep up on me when I least expected them. What I thought was a benign question would be a full out trigger for her. There's an old boxing expression about how the most dangerous punch there is—the one that'll knock you right on your ass—is the one that you don't see coming. That sentiment held true when it came to our fights, which were like that feint left hook that your eyes perceived about a nanosecond too late. Anna had a lot of those. Eventually I developed a type of reflex for them, like I could anticipate their occurrence with some degree of accuracy, but that particular skill set took some painful trial and error, the type that ended in a lot of apologizes and heart emoji's.

I was telling you about the first time though, right?

Remember those friends I mentioned before? Anna had this small but loyal group of friends she hung out with, kids she was tight with going way back to elementary school. Good kids, I'm sure, but not my friends by any stretch, I wouldn't have known much of their existence even if ran into them on the way to science. I didn't mention them in here because they honestly were never part of my life. I didn't hang out with them, we didn't interact outside of an occasional 'what's up', and Anna rarely said shit about them when we were together.

One afternoon I sent Anna my usual 'good morning beautiful' text (imagine a blushing smiley and heart emoji at the end of the sentence if you wanna picture it right). I asked her if she wanted to hang out after school for a little —maybe go to the rocks or something. She texted me back the she couldn't, 'cause she's going out after school. *Where*, I asked? Okay, now it's important to identify where shit goes sideways in a conversation—in my opinion, that exact moment, the starting pistol of our first fight, began with her reply to my text. *It's irrelevant, why do you need to know that*, she said. Before we even get into what happened next, let me cut to the final act just so you have some clarity. . .there was nothing shady or weird going on. No other guy. No dealing of crystal blue meth as a side hustle. Didn't need time to have a mandatory meeting with her nonexistent parole officer, nothing dramatic like that.

I just reached a point where it didn't matter what was really going on, the secrecy bothered me too much to let go. I brought it up. I brought it up in a way that wasn't nice. The first time we had a legit fight I thought it was the end. Goodbye love, goodbye happiness, it was great getting to know you, have fun wherever you're off to, send postcards so I can see how happy I'm not. Seriously. Curtains. Devolution. Tears and words that hurt. It was about the last thing I had ever envisioned happening to us, but there we were, regardless.

When you look back on these things after the fact they're always more clear than they were when you were in the fog of it all. In the absence of someone yelling at you, you can actually reflect on your own silly bullshit that led you to that point. Pettiness. Aggression. Insecurity. These are the people in your neighborhood. All that clarity shit is for later on, though. In the midst of all those emotions there's no introspection, there's only war to be waged in Pettiness's name.

What was it even over? Nothing. Teenaged bullshit. Jealously. Nothing that ever mattered as much as what actually mattered—how much we loved one another. How quickly that sentiment found its place on the back-burner. *Why were you talking to him? Oh, you're texting your ex? How long has that been going on? Wait, what? He told you he still has feelings for you? Does he know you have a boyfriend? And you didn't tell me this why? Oh, okay, sure, you say it's over but how do I know? Yeah I trust you, but. . .yeah I know what trust means, but you think he's not gonna try some shit? What do you mean 'so what if he does'? Are you crazy? No, I didn't mean like that, I'm sorry.*

Before I had a girlfriend I believed that I would have been a better boyfriend than all those douche bags I saw who got the girls and treated them like shit. I used to see them in the hallways, and think in my most acute self-right-eousness that I was better than those guys. I thought that jealously was beyond me, that I was too good for it, but you don't know who you are until you're in a situation. I was capable of some next-level insecurity when it came to Annalise, but that was my inexperience. I had no reps, no muscle memory. I had no experience to be confident in. Instead, I was like a poor person who found a suitcase full of money that everyone knew I'd found. I didn't know what to do with it, and I was scared that someone would inevitably try to take it from me.

After our tense exchange there was nothing. Radio silence. Unreturned texts followed up with panicked calls. It was predictable teen bedlam, but when she wouldn't return my texts I knew that things had gone wronger than wrong. She never cut me off. Never went more than fifteen minutes without returning a text. I don't remember how many times I actually typed that I was sorry, but it must have been a lot because every text after that, when I began an s-word my phone auto-filled the word *sorry*.

It didn't matter how many times I wrote that I was sorry, they all went unanswered, as did the calls and voice-mails I left practically begging her to answer me back. Two days isn't that long when measured on the continuum of human history, but in teenage relationship years it was an unbearable eternity. You all know what a panic attack is, right? Seen it on TV maybe, or read an article in the psychology section of the *New York Times*, something like that? Well if that's your reference, then understand that you know nothing, Jon Snow, and that real life mental illness made manifest is frightening—the sort that leaves you changed for having been its witness. I had my first one in my room, when all this went down. Thought I was dying. Thought Mom would be the one to find my body in my room and freak out. Turns out it was just anxiety. That was my first introduction to that type of thing, but the stress of the situation was starting to get to me physically.

So after two whole days of trying to contact Annalise, my mind looked like the lawn of that weird guy who lives at the end of every block in America; like that house that Pennywise lives in in *IT*, the one whose grass is about as tall as you were, with gnats and mosquitos circling the air, and a foul, nondescript odor always lingering. That was my brain without Anna—an absolute mess of an existence. I did my best to distract from my growing anxiety, but nothing quite fulfilled its internet-based promise of relaxation and stillness of mind. In turn, I tried the following home remedies:

<u>Yoga</u>: now if you think I actually went to a yoga class you're just a plain old silly goose. No way, man. Not into the mutual sweating and chanting on little expensive carpets while injuring myself, but I found some videos online that didn't look too hard. It was quite the realization to discover that there's literally no such thing as easy yoga. And, while I gained a newfound respect for people who did that shit for real, the strained contorting and the vertigo-induced breathing left me anything but relaxed. Which brings us to...

<u>Breathing techniques</u>: I found this article claimed to be written by a former navy seal, talking all about the breathing techniques he used to stay calm under the extreme pressure of assassinating or kidnapping whoever-the-fuck in some country no American could locate on a map. He called it 'box breathing' I think - basically even intervals of inhalation, holding your breath, and exhalation. If by calm this dude meant that I'd pass out from being light headed, and wouldn't notice my anxiety, well then he was onto something.

I tried everything I came across to relieve my anxiety, but nothing worked. Only one thing would work, and I knew that I had to talk to her, to work it out somehow, it was just a matter of getting her to answer me. From there I knew that I could talk to her. It was Sunday morning when I decided to make one final, heartfelt attempt. I knew that another 'I'm sorry, please answer me' text wasn't going to do anything (*what was that old expression about the definition of insanity*). I decided to use the only tool I ever really had—my words.

The words really did visit me, but maybe that's not the right way to say it. More like the words always existed—they were like some omniscient entity that resided in a part of my brain that wasn't accessible whenever I wanted it to be. That place wasn't a room that I had the key for, it was more like a museum that had some very specific hours of operation. I could go there, sometimes, but never at pure will. There were always parameters, and most of the time I just had to wait, wait for the words to be audible to me, then all I had to do was get them recorded so they could live forever. I knew even then that the writer's greatest tool was his ability to listen to his own voice. That was true enough. But sometimes, in a bind, you had to push it; you had to bang the shit out of the museum door, even if it was after-hours, and demand to be let in.

I thought of where we began, and then it became as clear as day. The rocks. Our rocks. The place we never left. The place where there was no jealousy, no pettiness. There were places like that, I realized, places that were so essential to goodness that they had this force field around them; this thin but effective layer of human memory that guarded everything inside that bubble, and wouldn't let anything bad penetrate, no matter what. Sometimes we found those places, and sometimes we created them. Anna and I had one, and I needed to go there to write the words down.

I remembered the route without directions, as if the car knew where to go and I was just the mindless, heartbroken kid at the helm. Twenty minutes after I left I was there. I parked in a spot—not our spot but one on the same side—and sat staring at the rocks. There were people everywhere, but it didn't matter. I just starred, waiting to hear that voice, the one that would tell me all the right words to get her back. Ten minutes passed with no sound but the distant laughter and crashing of water against rocks. And then, out of nowhere, the words.

It's strange to be here without you. It's a beautiful day; the wind rushes across my face carrying the smell of the water in its gust. From here the bridge decorates the horizon, hovering over the water as hundreds of cars fly by in the distance. As I watch the small moving dots speed by I think how little they know of this place. Most of them probably make this trip every morning, speeding by with eyes faced forward and coffee cups filling their hands. This is just another day for them. They drive by in masses, perhaps not even glancing to their right to see what must look to them a single line of tiny little stones carving a strip through the water. They have no idea what they drive over every day, but we do.

They travel over sacred ground, woefully ignorant of its significance. Maybe that's all the better, because this is our place, and its place in Our Story is only meant for us to know. This is where it all began; chronologically not very long ago, but really years ago when measured in what we mean to each other. This geography has become some of the most significant of my life. This place is a part of you, and now you're forever a part of me.

As I sit here I watch the wind bend the reeds over towards the west, and even with just the crack of my car windows I'm reminded of how cold it is here. Not cold to you, of course, but cold to me. The sensation would normally be aversive,

but this particular discomfort brings with it the strongest sense memories and when I feel the shiver manifest in goosebumps on my arm, I look over and I can see us there. I'm looking at the spot now, as a group of teenaged boys yell and race each other over the spot where we first sat and talked. I was so cold. But I can't feel that cold right now, all my mind can process is the memory of you on my left, sitting down on the stones, your hair blowing around as you told me deeply personal stories about your life and your pain. I remember the tone of your voice so clearly.

The view is amazing, but it's just not the same without you. This particular view is meant to be shared. This is our view. You told me that when you come here alone you listen to music and try to forget the pain that brought you here in the first place, but I'm here to remember. Part of me wants to reach over to roll up the windows, but I won't. The breeze forces its way inside the car, and I can see us there, as if I'm watching a film of us. There we are: me poorly dressed for the occasion, and you, your deep brown eyes fixed at an angle to my right, off in the distance, as I listened to your story.

I can smell your hair and I can hear you humming—I love when you hum—your long black boots pressed up against the front of my car, and your eyes once again at an angle into the distance. Another strong breeze rushes over the right side of my body. The wind came from that direction the first time we were here, freezing my right ear and pushing your hair about your face as you spoke. We didn't stay on the actual rocks very long at all.

The longer I sit here the more people pass in front of me: women pushing their babies in strollers; old men with their walking partners; grandmothers babysitting their grandchildren, and joggers breathing heavily as they bounce by with headphones in. All of them pass by where we sat that day, and none of them know Our Story, but maybe one day they will.

I'm remembering, writing, and thinking of you, and those things are inexorably linked in a triad, which is to say that they don't exist separately, but come together to allow me to write words like these, as my thumbs start to cramp from writing so much. I perceive the pain but I don't really feel it, what I feel is that day when you leaned your head on my shoulder for the first time. I feel the tickle of your hair against my face as we kissed, and the sensation of your fingers running over my arm.

It was then that I learned how much your kiss reveals about you. Your kiss *is* you, and maybe that's why I ache to never go too long without it. I don't love kissing you just because it invokes some physical response, but because everything that you are is transmitted in it. When we kiss we're alone together, ghosts to the world around us, and locked away in each other's hearts. Your kiss is us.

I didn't have any grand conclusion, but that's what was in my heart to write. I thought that baring my soul would be enough, that it would remind her of how silly this fight was, and send her running back to me, begging me for more words. But when was it ever that simple? Oh, right, never. Never ever. Did you see it going any other way? Like, me having this epiphany, driving to the rocks, writing my little whatever, then Anna running back into my arms? Hope, right? For suckers. The words worked. They did something, because after I wrote them she texted me back, finally, after two solid days of not speaking.

ELEVEN

Where I can't stop the momentum of her loss.

Remember the movie *American Beauty*, where Lester, the main character and narrator, tells you in the opening line that he'll be dead by the end of the movie? There were probably still people surprised at the ending, demanding their money back from the goofy high school kid who only took the job at the theater for the free popcorn. Even when you try to warn people they still get surprised. I guess it's human nature to want a happy ending, but the opposite of a happy ending isn't a devastating ending. The opposite of a happy ending is the truth. Real life.

The nuclear annihilation that I had stupidly wished on the Peruvian people when Anna was on her way there came back to me twofold. Ground Zero was my car. I believe that somewhere, wherever that car is today, if you look closely you can see my nuclear shadow still burned into the driver seat. After I poured my heart out to her in that letter she actually texted me back that specific combination of words which, to my mind, have never done anything but inspire anxiety in all who've heard them: *I need to talk to you.* My heart sunk when I read them on my phone. I pretended to be less panicked than I was, and just wrote back that I was free now if she wanted to talk. Of course, she said, come get me. I'll be right there, I told her. Which do you want first, the bad news or the bad news?

My heart stated racing during what you can imagine was the worst drive ever. Lamb to the slaughter, only with the consciousness that the slaughter is coming. I pulled up in front of her house, the house she shared with two other families, and looked around. Normally I was so focused on her that the rest of the world kind of melted around me. I didn't notice the little things around Annalise, only her. But that day, as I waited for her to come out and break my heart, I looked around. This part of the neighborhood might as well have been another neighborhood entirely. It was like a museum to the messed up housing of suburbia. This is where she's from, I thought. This is where she needs to get away from, isn't it?

Anna came out of the house with no phone, and I had the weirdest memory. I remembered that scene in The Godfather where Don Corleone tells Michael that whoever comes to him to arrange the meeting is the traitor, and to always remember that. That's what I thought of when she said we had to talk, and that's what I thought of again when I saw her walking towards the car. This time it was just her, wrapped in an oversized light grey hoodie, leggings, and those black boots I'll always remember her wearing. She jumped in the passenger side, her eyes red either from crying, not sleeping, or maybe both. I'd learned not to ask, and I already knew a little bit about the craziness she lived in everyday, so instead I just leaned over and kissed her. When she gave me that cousin-peck instead of a boyfriend kiss I knew this was it, all that was left was to go through the motions.

"Hey," I said.

"Potato. Can we drive somewhere?"

"Yeah, of course. Where do you want to go? The Rocks?"

"No," she said sharply. "Not there. Anywhere but. You pick, just go."

"Alright."

I didn't know many places to go, so I went to the giant, oversized parking lot of the grocery store that had opened in our town the previous year. It was just a grocery store like Lance Armstrong was just a good cyclist. What I mean to say is that it was a mega-mart, a giant corporate chair store on its third cycle of Human Growth Hormone, where you could do just about everything except your taxes. The parking lot was accordingly ridiculous. You could have housed a third of America's homeless population inside its perimeter, so I chose the farthest spot from the store so we could have some privacy. I needed it, and I only hoped that no one was around to see what was about to happen. What threw me off was that she just started crying. Bawling. Movie shit. The fact that there was no warning, paired with the fact that she was never that vulnerable, threw me for a weird loop, and I instinctually reached my arm around her shoulder to comfort her. "What's the matter? What is it?"

"I'm sorry," she said. She said it again and again, broken words spoken though a sobbing face, but I made them out just fine. I knew what the sorry meant. I knew that she wasn't apologizing for cutting me off, or for our fight, or the things she'd said. She was apologizing for breaking up with me, which she had yet to officially do. Like I said, we understood one another, in love and in tragedy. "I can't do this anymore. I just can't."

"It's okay," I told her, rubbing her back. I don't know

why my first thought was to make her feel better when I was the one getting hurt, but that's how I was with her, and I could see the pain it was causing her to have to do this.

"Don't lie," she said. "Don't tell me it's okay when it's not."

"Look at me," I told her, and I did it with a confident command in my voice I honestly didn't know existed until I used it in that moment, but it worked. She looked up at me with those tear soaked brown eyes, and I had to fight to hold back tears of my own. "You're right, it's not okay. Not at all. But no matter what, I don't want you to be sad." I was telling the truth when I said that, mostly because the whole thing hadn't hit me yet. But besides that, there were types of love just like there were types of beauty, and in my hierarchy of loves the selfless ones stood squarely at the top of that pyramid. Those are the loves that care more about the other person than yourself, and that's what I felt for Annalise. I never wanted anything from her. I only wanted to give her what she wanted. But I couldn't do that. So I guess my love was like that fighter who loses on the score-cards but still comes across like the moral victor because he gave such a valiant and stupidly brave effort. That was my first love. A moral victory.

"There's no helping that," she said. "Not now, not ever." I could hear the depressed voice, the *Bleh*, I knew it better than any seventeen year old should have.

"Can I ask why?"

"I'm moving," she said. It was the first I'd heard of anything like that, and it was about the last thing I expected to hear.

"Moving? Where?"

"Peru," she said, and my heart dropped again. There was moving and then there was MOVING. I stupidly thought she meant that she was going away to college, and before she spoke I was ready to counter with the naive 'we can make it work' speech, but those hopes had been shattered instantly with the name of a single country spoken out loud.

"When?"

"Next week," she said.

"What!"

"I can't stay at my house anymore, Logan, I just can't. It isn't you, and it isn't us. I need to get away from her and that's the only option. My family there said they'd take me."

"But I don't get it," I said, totally confused. "Why so suddenly? You're not even going to finish out the year?"

"I know this will be hard for you to understand, but I have to save myself. She wants me to go, and it's something I have to do. I. . .I hurt myself for the first time in a year."

"You did what? When?"

"Yesterday," she told me. "I'm not proud of it, okay. I'm not happy about it. In fact, I'm depressed as hell, but Mom and I had another bad fight. We've been having those almost every day." *Every day*, I thought, she never told me about them. But I stopped asking questions once I realized that this wasn't what she wanted, it was what she needed. She needed to get out of this place, she needed to get out of that home before it ruined her forever.

"I love you," I said.

"Potato."

"I wish that was enough."

I clutched her head and put it against my chest, and I could feel the dampness of her tears and the warmth of her face through my shirt. How long we sat like that I couldn't tell you. Even with the distance of time I get too choked up in my own memories to accurately remember, but we sat there a while. There were more words spoken, of course. More apologies, more declarations of love, more assertions that she never meant to hurt me. Promises that we'd still keep in touch. Breakups 101, right? But for me it was a cut so deep that I didn't even bleed. Didn't feel the blade. I was eviscerated. My body just hadn't fallen over yet.

I drove Anna back to that place she was willing to skip the country to escape. We weren't going to drag this out any longer than necessary, we both agreed. We broke up then and there, and it wasn't until I saw her walking away from me that I cried. I felt it coming like a sudden pressure, and then my tear ducts did their thing, and I felt like I might never be okay again. I sat there for a few minutes in front of her house because I didn't want to drive while I was like that, but then I decided that I looked crazy and needed to continue my break down in a more private place, like my room.

That night I wrote. There were no more love letters or sweet sentiments left in me, at least there wouldn't be for good long while, but I still had my thoughts. I'd always wanted to be a writer, ever since I was a little kid. Anna had woken up that dormant dream in me by being my muse, my inspiration, my focus for the feelings coursing through my body when I was with her. But just as quickly she'd shut them down, and I was left with an all new *Bleh* —a mutant one that blended sadness, anger, confusion, resentment and, strangest of all, understanding and acceptance. It was the last part that was the weirdest to deal with. I should have just been heartbroken and pissed off— and I was—but that selfless love let me understand that maybe this was the best thing for her.

And then I had a weird thought. What if someone could have saved mom from her abusive house when she was a teen? What if she could have flown to Puerto Rico and gone to college there? I mean, yeah, I wouldn't exist, but that hypothetical kept echoing in my mind. Anna was just like Mom, only she had time. And once I had that thought, my anger melted away temporarily, and all I felt was that love. It didn't matter what I wanted because I needed Annalise to be happy, even if that happiness didn't include me.

Maybe deep down I knew this would end badly, but how could I resist her? How could anyone resist her? Long jet black hair, the most beautiful brown eyes you've ever seen in your damn life! It was great for that short while in which things are allowed to be great, what you might stereotypically call the 'honeymoon phase', and then everything soured. The reasons don't even matter, do they? I should have known that I was going to lose the best thing that's ever happened to me, and there wasn't a damn thing in this world I could have done to slow the momentum of her loss. I saw it play out, like a short film in high definition, played in fast forward and slow motion at the same time. The saddened narrator, some James Earl Jones type character, spoke in my mind while images of me and her played before my eyes while I sat in my room. The narrator said,

You'll lose her to There, wherever There might be. She'll go, not because she doesn't love you, and not because she wants to cause you pain, but because Here is where all the hurt resides; it lives like an invisible tenant in her crowded house, like a guest who never pays rent but is always on time for dinner. Here is where the pain gets remembered, the walls of that shitty little place a mental tapestry of past injustices and traumas. Here is where she becomes just another girl who stays too long and works down the avenue, maybe serving

coffee for a few years longer than a girl should serve coffee. Here is where that old mirror, the one she got for her birthday that hangs behind her door, reflects a face that's still undeniably beautiful, but getting too old to be appreciated by any man who matters anymore.

Her husband, who she hasn't met yet, will be the one to tell her she's beautiful, something she hears all the time from the assholes she pours coffee for, but she never believes because she knows that even if she were a straight up dog with two moles and yellow teeth they'd all still try to get with her. But this man, the nice man, he's different. He means it when he says she's beautiful, and she knows that because the last time someone told her that sincerely she was a young girl with a bright future, and pretty girls with bright futures can take compliments for granted, because they know that more will surely come from an endless parade of boys. Then the boys become men, creepy men with bad intentions, and the falsehood of those same words that all the handsome boys used to throw at her is perceptible, but it doesn't stop her from pretending they're real. Maybe she needs to pretend, needs to believe in their sincerity. Maybe she needs that so bad she lets the least creepy ones get on top of her from time to time, like she knows they want to, and as he's on top of her, thrusting downward in a clumsy and rough way, she thinks that maybe the smell of him is worth it, even if only for an evening of feeling loved.

At least someone still wants her, even if it's just for a body tight enough to make the men feel

like they're with a young woman. Even if they appreciate what's between her legs more than they recognize the glimmer you saw in her big brown eyes. Well, so what? What's so wrong with that? Who decided long ago that the world has to be a fair place anyway? Suckers, that's who. Suckers who believe in hope because that's who hope is for; the dumb, romantic ones who were raised by happy parents who read them fairy tales before tucking them into their warm beds. Those same people wouldn't dare drive through this neighborhood or stop in to eat at her diner. You see, those people don't live Here; they don't send their kids to these schools, or allow them to hang out on these cold streets, so who gives a shit about their romantic notions, anyhow?

And then, in some weird psychedelic moment, like a vision of the future that I saw so vividly that it scared me, I heard the rest of the story in Anna's voice. Only it wasn't the same Anna. She was old, worn, inexorably distorted, but it was still her. In this vision I saw an alternative life, as though she'd stayed in her neighborhood instead of going to Peru, and I was listening to her voice as if she was whispering in my ear. I've never had a moment like that since that one, but it was so real that I can hear her like she was next to me. She said,

I may not get all that I want, or even all that I deserve, but I'll live. People talk about surviving all the time, but I say I'll live instead. It's not the life I saw myself having, but it's a life like my mother before me, and maybe my daughter after me. I met this nice man, he always tells me how pretty I am, and he means it. I can tell the difference, you know, I've had my share of bad guys, but this one isn't like the others, he means it when he says I'm beautiful. He'll make all the difference. He'll have a decent job, and he'll smell nice, and he may be friends with some of those assholes at the diner, but he won't be one of them. He'll be. . .different. And he'll make me different because when he gets on top of me he'll say that he loves me first, he'll remind me how beautiful he thinks I am. He'll say sweet things.

Maybe I won't even mind because maybe it'll actually feel good for once; feel clean, feel like I'm not just a warm body to be used, lying on my back and staring at the ceiling, counting the minutes until it's over so I can go into the bathroom and clean myself up. I don't want babies but I don't believe in birth control—better not to mess with God's plan, like my Mom always told me. But this nice man, he says he loves me, and that I'm beautiful, and that it feels too good to stop, and not to worry because if he were to plant a baby inside of me, we'd get married and he'd stay forever.

That's what happens Here. Here is where all this goes down, like a storm nobody's got the power to stop. I'm living Here, and I'll live here until I'm not living any more. It's okay. It's okay. Bad things happen to good people, right? That's what my mom used to tell me. I'd tell her to stop being negative, but now I know she's right—moms are always right, even when they're wrong. I'll tell Mariela—that'll be my baby girl's name one day— I'll tell her the same, maybe even sooner. She should know that bad things happen early, this way she won't be disappointed later with all that hope bullshit, 'cause hope is for suckers, and I'm not raising any suckers. She'll live Here too, but she'll do better than I did, I know she will. I'll raise her better than I was raised—with or without her father, that nice man who meant it when he called me beautiful—the one who actually felt good on top of me, and promised to come back from his business trip a month ago. I know he'll be back, because he was so nice, so sincere. I'm late on my period but I'm not worried, I've got the baby of a good man inside me and a promise that he'll be back soon.

I may be ordinary, but her father is different, and maybe some of that difference can pass to her, and she can be at least half different from the other girls—from me—and then maybe she can get away, she can live over There, somewhere. But if not then she can live Here too, until she stops living at all, and has a daughter of her own. We are living. We're living Here, until we don't live anymore.

I opened my eyes and tears rolled down my face, and I knew that I'd done the right thing, the selfless thing, by not fighting Anna. I needed her, but as it turned out, she needed me even more. Life was funny in that way. And in the same way that our relationship began by email and text, so too did it end that way. I knew that I probably shouldn't have, but I texted her after my vision because I needed some sense of closure.

"You know I'll never love anyone the way I love you."

"I'm sorry that I'm so screwed up," she wrote back. "I'm sorry if I screwed you up, too, because you don't deserve that. I know you're dealing with a lot already. I wish things were different."

"Maybe these are some of the last words we say. I

don't know. But if they are, don't ever apologize for how you feel, and don't worry about me. I'll miss you like a part of me has been amputated, but I understand."

"Potato," she wrote.

"Ditto," I wrote back. It was my way around her rule. It was clever, if I do say so myself.

What I did next shocked me more than Annalise breaking up with me. To those reading this who come from happy homes it might not seem a big deal, but it was something revolutionary. In the short span of a few years I'd gotten used to being an emotional orphan. The people who were my parents still lived and breathed, but for all emotional intents and purposes they both died when I was fifteen. I couldn't talk to them, I couldn't confide in them, I couldn't even get yelled at or punished by them. I was alone, and I'd gotten used to that condition. But despite how well I thought I handled having my heart ripped out, Aztec-sacrifice style, I was feeling a type of pain that I didn't know existed. I wasn't anxious and I wasn't depressed, I was hurt like that kid who falls off the top of the turtle statue in the park and hits his head. I needed comfort.

I put my phone down because I didn't want to see it for a while, and I opened the door to my room. I knew Mom would be downstairs in her chair because that's always where she was. Only I wasn't going down to check on her like I normally did, I was going down because I needed her. The chair she used to sit in was huge, bigger than her ninety pound body could fit, and usually those gaps between her and the end of the chair got filled with blankets, or sometimes pillows from our couch, but that day I did the job. I didn't say a word, because sometimes words just got in the way. I passed in front of our TV, nuzzled myself next to my mom like I was a little boy, even though I was twice her size, and cried.

For once my tears weren't for anyone else. I wasn't crying for my mom or dad, for my hatred of school, or for things I wish I had. I was crying because I was sad and I needed my mom, and for the first time in a long time our roles were put back into their natural order, and she became my parent again. She didn't say much, because she also knew when words got in the way. I let her comfort me because in that moment it was okay to be selfish, and the feeling of having my pain understood was enough to take away some of its power. "It's okay, baby," she said to me. "Whatever it is. It'll be okay."

"I know," I said softly. "And ditto, Mom. Ditto."

TWELVE

Where I have lunch with my best friend one more time.

The diner was our spot. It was every kid's spot, so saying that it was our spot was hardly original, but this is my story, so I can say it was ours. That was the place we met to be best friends, and so that's where I wanted to go the day after Annalise broke my heart. I was having a better day than I thought I would, all things considered. I mean, by all media accounts I should have been devastated—and I was—but I wasn't depressed-in-bed devastated. Maybe that's because I saw it coming for a while, even though I wouldn't allow myself to consciously admit it. I called Pete last night after I sat with Mom for a while, and he told me he'd take me out for lunch. That was a very Pete thing to do. He was weirdly comforting like that.

I got there first and got the booth we usually sat in. I hadn't brought my phone. We were fighting. That shit needed to stay face down on my nightstand where I left it. Any messages or notifications could wait until I was back to my normal existence. It was weird to sit and exist without scrolling through a phone. That must have been what it was like when my parents were kids. Crazy. Pete wasn't too late. And by not too late I mean only like ten or fifteen minutes, but I was estimating because who could tell without a phone? "Hey," he said. He was looking at me like someone had just died.

"Hey. I ordered you a Coke."

"Thanks, man, you're the best."

"Welcome."

"Do you know that I've never peed in the shower?"

"What? Jesus, that was the most random thing you've ever said to me. What are you talking about?"

"Am I strange?"

"For saying shit like that out of the blue? Yeah, very."

"No, seriously," he reiterated. "Do you pee in the shower?"

"Doesn't everyone?"

"Apparently. Talk about the things no one tells you. I peed in the shower for the first time before I came here. It was a transformative experience."

"I think you peed out your last brain cells. What's your obsession with shower peeing?"

"It started at the hotel in the city. I'm sorry for bringing that up, but you asked."

"It's okay. Go on."

"Well Lindsey and I obviously don't live together."

"Obviously."

"So we never shared a bathroom or shower before. When we were staying over she told me that she pees in the shower. I have to be honest, man, it changed the way I look at her."

"You're insane. Lindsey's the best thing that ever happened to you. You're going to marry that girl one day, trust me. You can't look at her different because she does something everyone in the world does. She should have looked at you different."

"Well I thought I was the weird one, so I decided to try it this morning. I have to tell you, it's over rated. I could have waited until I got out. It freaked me out a little."

"I'm sorry you had that experience."

"Shit. I know, I'm being selfish and insensitive, aren't I?"

"It's actually really amusing, so if you have any other random or weird shit to say I'm all ears. It would be a welcome respite from talking about last night."

Pete got serious when I said that. For all his silliness he was about as solid as a friend got; a rock when I needed just that. "I feel like I keep telling you that I'm sorry, and I know that doesn't mean anything right now."

"It means more than you think."

"Well, then, I'm sorry. You don't deserve any more pain. Are you mad?"

"Actually, strangely, I'm not. Or maybe I'm just in denial and I'll be really pissed and bitter in a little while, but for right now I'm okay. I can't bring myself to be mad at her."

"Well that's nice of you. I'd be pissed as hell."

"It's nobody's fault," I said, reflecting back. "She didn't do anything wrong and neither did I. It just. . ."

"Wasn't meant to be?"

"No," I said. "It was totally meant to be. But not everything that's meant to be is meant to last. Everything ends. That doesn't mean it wasn't the best thing that ever happened to me."

"Look at you."

"What?" I asked.

"A relationship virgin no more. Your first heartbreak

and you're handling it like the old soul that Mom always called you."

"Who would've guessed? I thought I'd be catatonic after something like this."

"You're strong. You always have been. Whether you wanted to be or not, it's the truth. You'll be fine."

"I've heard that somewhere before," I said.

"So I hate to ask, but what's her deal?"

"Anna?"

"Yeah. Is it going to be weird seeing her every day?"

"I'm not going to be seeing her," I said. "She's moving, like ASAP."

"Moving? Where?"

"Peru. She has family there."

"Yeah, I remember. Why?"

I didn't know how to answer that question. It was a good question, one that a best friend should ask, but I didn't want to betray any of the private things Annalise and I had shared, even though we weren't together anymore. The real answer was too long and too complex to exchange over a plate of mozzarella fries, even if I had been inclined to get into it. She needed an escape; she needed a new start. . .

"She needed to get away from here, I guess."

"Well who doesn't?"

"That's a great question my friend. I wish I had an answer for you."

"You know what I wish?"

"What's that?"

"I wish I knew why people liked peeing in the shower."

"Not sure," I said. "But if you even think of throwing one of those fries at me I'm gonna start punching you. I'm not sure when I'll stop."

We laughed and got back to just being friends and

talking about the dumb, random stuff that only best friends in high school can talk about. It was the best way I could have spent the afternoon after losing the girl of my dreams. A plate of mozzarella fries and a Coke didn't make the pain go away, but it was a damn fine start.

Things were going to be okay. I'd live.

Epilogue

_____

Where I realize something I should have realized a very long time ago.

So what happened? That's what you're all wondering, right? You're probably like, *Logan, you just left your sad, seventeen year old, college bound, broken-hearted self eating fries at a diner, talking about peeing in the shower. What the hell happened after all that?* A lot happened of course, too much to put here with any degree of detail that does those things justice, but I'll give you the bullet points of what you want to know.

Pete and Lindsey got married, can you believe that? I mean, what high school relationship ever lasted past those two weeks after graduation where the respective parties just refused to admit it was over? Exactly none that I've ever heard of. But that's my Boy, he always had a way of making things happen for himself. I never say corny stuff like this, but those two were meant for one another. They got their romantic comedy, pop-song-in-the-background life, and I couldn't be happier for them. Working on their second baby right now and struggling for a name. I, of course, suggested Logan, but that decision is still pending. I'll keep you posted.

What about Mom? Good days, bad days. Functional years and not-so-functional years. Ups and downs, war and peace. Depression 101. I told you that she was a fighter though, and that's where I got my scrap from. Nothing, not even Depression, can just be insurmountably bad forever. She fought the *Bleh* something awful for years and she still fights it to this day. Only now she wins some rounds. Last I checked the score was 10-8 in favor of the *Bleh*, but it's a back and forth bout. She lives on her own in that same house I grew up in back in the neighborhood. She takes daily walks and volunteers at the local library on days when she can be around people. We talk all the time, and not just about mental illness stuff. We talk-talk. Mother and son stuff. *How's it going? What are you working on? What's your next book going to be about?* That kind of stuff. It's nowhere near perfect, but that's how life goes. It's our version of normal, finally.

And. . .drumroll, please. What happened to Annalise? I'd love to sit here and tell you a happy story about how she's doing, how she kept her demons at bay and fixed all the problems in her life. I'd love to tell you that, but the truth is, I really don't know. She really did leave for Peru in the middle of the year. No prom, no graduation ceremony, no storybook ending to an otherwise illustrious high school career. None of that. A few months later I was gone, too, accepted at Boston University and dorming with dudes who say *KA* when they meant to say *car*. Vowels for days. We texted once or twice, mostly with me asking how she was doing and getting something vague in return days later, and then I stopped. That's how it goes sometimes. The people we love the most exit stage left, never to return, but that doesn't mean they didn't leave a mark. It doesn't mean that they didn't change us for the better.

I told her once that even if the world around her was blind, that I still saw everything that mattered. She said that I was different, and that it scared her. I wish she'd known that she was the different one, and I was so very ordinary. I was just a boy. A boy madly and hopelessly in love. I wish she'd known that when I finally mustered the strength to talk to her that day, that I only looked alive, but that I was really in the middle of drowning in a sadness so deep that it almost took me away forever, and that loving her had saved my life in ways she could never understand. Oh well. At least she'll always have my words.

So much about Annalise was a contrast: her sweetness and her temper; her openness and the fortress walls she put up around her heart; the illumination her smile could create, and the sadness her tears could inspire. She was as much of a mystery to me as she was the person who knew me best, and maybe she wanted to stay that way forever. Maybe being a mystery was a safe place where no evil could ever find you. It was a place her mom didn't have the key to, a place that had no coordinates. I've let go of the pain and the resentment because, well, it was a long time ago, and the differences between a seventeen year old and a grown man should be severe enough to understand at least a little bit about why people are the way they are. That's what maturity gives you. That's what distance gives you. That's what time gives you.

But if you're ready for my last, and weirdest, thought on this matter, I'd love to share it with you. After all, why would I stop now, I've told you every other damn thought I had, so maybe you'll stay with me for one more. When I look back at that time I always wonder about the potato thing. There was so much else going on that I never got the full meaning of the word when she used it, but I think now I do. Potato was *I'm mad*, Potato was *I don't know how to tell you my sadness*; potato was *I'm gonna confuse you 'cause it makes me laugh*. Potato was Annalise—complex as hell, and something you needed time to understand fully. But in seeing all that, I missed its most important meaning. I missed it then, and I didn't even realize it until just now. And it's so simple that my overly analytical self never bothered to decode the message she was trying to give.

Potato was *I love you*.

It was *I love you* when *I love you* couldn't be said out loud. Damn.

But don't despair. Dry your eyes. We end on a good note. These days are good days, ones where the words that always eluded me get put down on paper and actually stay there. No self-doubt, no thinking I'm no good at expressing myself. Anna always told me that I was a good writer, and that I should write for more people than just her. Well, I did. I wrote my first novel, a love story (what else?), and I'm going to publish it soon. It's about Us, about Our Story. I don't know what I'm going to call it, or if anyone's even going to care enough to read it, but that doesn't matter. What matters is that I did it. All books need to have a dedication, right? The inspiration for the story. Well, that one is obvious to the point of insulting your intelligence, so instead of saying it, I'll just leave it for you to read.

To Annalise

I don't know where you are or what you're doing. Maybe you're chilling on a Peruvian beach with a good looking dude named Juan, cradling those gorgeous babies I always knew you'd make (hell, how could your babies not be beautiful, do you not remember how you look?), or maybe you came home after a few weeks and started working at the diner pouring coffee. I don't know. Maybe I'll never know. But wherever you are, I wrote Our Story, Anna! I finally did it. I always joked that I'd tell this to people one day because Our Story was worth telling, and you said encouraging things about how well I used my words, and how I should write for more people than just you. Well, like with so many things, you were right. You were right in that way that only you could be. And whether or not you actually thought I'd ever do this, you helped me believe in myself at a time when that was still a rare thing.

If I'm being honest—and really, was I ever anything but honest with you, even when I didn't want to be—it's been weird to revisit Us. It's been everything that we were: so right, so wrong. So simple, and so very, very complicated. But the truth is that I love my painful remembering; I love those emotions that only come to be when I think back on that time. People get that wrong, you know. They say (that damn *Council of They* again!). . . They say that there's only one way to experience love. Well, as you once pointed out to me, the *Council of They* is full of shit. The way I loved you is not the way I've ever loved anyone else, and that doesn't make our love better than any other, but it does make it unique; it does make my love for you a one of a kind, limited edition, variant cover signed by the artist. That was us.

So wherever you are, remember that you're always Here in these pages, and these pages don't exist in the print you hold, that's just an illusion, they exist inside me, a place you'll forever reside. I hope the cross I got you still sits on your heart so that you always remember me. But if not, here it is, all for you.

My book.

My love letter.
Our Story.
So, yeah. . .potato.

Five things I (re) discovered while writing Away From Here that I wanted to share with you.

---

1. Being vulnerable, and allowing yourself to be seen by others is a strength, not a weakness, even when that vulnerability causes intense pain.
2. It's okay to be sad sometimes, as long as it's a place you rent and not one you buy.
3. Our greatest powers and our deepest flaws are sometimes imperceptibly similar things, and all it takes is that realization to change how you see your condition in life.
4. Moms are the most important things in the world, maybe ever. Top 3 at least.
5. Best friends are like having a fire extinguisher in your house - they're not always needed, but when they are they're absolute lifesavers.

Author's Note

Where I invite you to tell your story.

This is a work of fiction based on some very real issues I dealt with when I was the age of the characters in the book. I guess if we're being honest, the issues of mental illness never fully go away, but hopefully they become more manageable. If you were/are a member of the Kids of Sick Parents club, I encourage you to tell your own story, to share your experiences with the world, and to always remember that there's a light at the end of the tunnel. I encourage everyone reading this to share their stories, as many others have done already, as a comment on my blog at www.authorchristopherharlan.com/blog. I'd love to read about your personal experiences with any of the themes in the book, which are things we all share as part of the human experience.